Hiding Out
Guardian Security Book Seven

by

Desiree Holt

Hiding Out

Cover Art by *Diana Carlile*

The Wild Rose Press, Inc.
PO Box 708
Adams Basin, NY 14410-0708
Visit us at www.thewildrosepress.com

Publishing History
First Edition, 2023
Trade Paperback ISBN 978-1-5092-5239-8
Digital ISBN 978-1-5092-5240-4

Previously Published 2015 by The Wild Rose Press
Published in the United States of America

Danger, despair, and desperation...
She's the only witness. He's her only hope.

Peering in at an angle, Robin saw Milla wringing her hands and backing away from the tall man looming over her. At six foot four, C.D. towered over his petite wife, who barely topped five feet. His angelic looks belied the devil that lurked beneath the surface.

"Oh? Is that it? Or did you sneak someone in here when Frank wasn't looking? Some guy, maybe?"

"C.D., you know—"

"I know you're a lying little bitch." He scanned the room. There was someone in here tonight, wasn't there?"

"No, no, I—"

The sound of the blow cut off the rest of the sentence. A crack sounded.

On the balcony, Robin flinched as if she'd taken the blow herself. Tears of rage filled her eyes.

She wanted to smash open the doors and hit C.D. with the handiest thing she could find. Anything to show him what pain was like. But she couldn't overpower C.D. and Frank both, and she didn't want to make things worse for Milla.

Worse? What a laugh. How much worse could the situation be?

Besides, she'd be no help to them if she was beaten to a bloody pulp. Or worse. She'd just have to hope that C.D. would expend his temper and leave. Then Robin would get Milla and Bobby out, even if she had to drag them by their hair.

In the meantime, it took all her willpower to do nothing.

Dedication

To Diana, whose patience and talent are jewels
in my life. Thank you for everything.

Chapter One

"Robin, you've got to take Bobby and get out of here. And I mean right now."

Robin Fletcher heard the note of desperation in her sister's voice as she pleaded with her. They were in the master bedroom of Milla's house—the McMansion, as Robin called it—and she couldn't help noting the fresh bruises on Milla's delicate complexion. Her sister had tried to hide the ones on her face with makeup, and by combing her long, dark hair forward. But they were so bad and her skin so translucent, the discolorations bled through the covering and were visible whenever her hair swung back. Robin was sure the long-sleeved blouse covered even more.

"It's too dangerous for both of you to keep living here one minute longer. And tonight is the perfect night to do it. Look at you," she went on. "You've got bruises on top of bruises. How long before he really snaps and kills you, for God's sake? Or Bobby?"

"He'd never hurt Bobby," Milla protested. "I protect him. Anyway, C.D. is so focused on having an heir to carry on his precious name, I don't think he'd jeopardize that."

"He's jeopardizing it now, damn it," Robin cried. "You think Bobby doesn't know what goes on in this house? How many times can you tell him you fell on the stairs or walked into a door? He may be only five years

1

old, but he's a smart kid. You know what he asked me?"

"I'm not sure I want to know."

"He asked me why his dad is so mean to his mom, and if that's why she hurts herself so much. He says his dad is a mean man."

Milla hugged herself and rubbed her hands up and down her arms, as if trying to warm herself. Her eyes, once a brilliant emerald green, were haunted now and had heavy shadows beneath them.

"I can handle it," she protested in a voice not quite steady. "Really. I can."

Robin snorted. "Yeah, right." Her voice softened to a pleading tone. "Milla, honey, do you know that every year almost four million women are abused by their partner?"

"That's why you've got to take Bobby and get out of here." Milla shifted nervously. "Robin, please—"

"And that abuse results in three deaths every day? Do you want to be one of those statistics?" God. She had to make her sister listen to her. She'd come here tonight on a mission, and she wasn't leaving until it was successful.

"You don't understand." Milla twisted her fingers together.

"No, I don't. Please let me call Zander. He'll know what to do. He can help us."

Zander Craig was a top agent with Guardian Security, one of the high-level security agencies in the country based out of San Antonio, Texas. Robin had known him for a long time, before he left Seattle to join Guardian. They had dated for a long while, and an intense relationship had grown between them. But when he moved to San Antonio and tried to get her to go with him, she had walked away. Things were so bad with Milla and Bobby, she felt she couldn't leave them. But now, his name was the first one that came to mind. Regardless of how he felt about their breakup, she was sure he'd answer her call for help. That was just who he was.

"No one can help us. Anyway, you haven't spoken to the man since he left Seattle. How do you know he'll even take your call, the way things ended?"

"I just know." And she did. They'd had something special, and she'd turned her back on it. But she had a feeling the connection was still there. Anyway, he was the only one she trusted in this situation.

She studied her sister.

"What is it, anyway? Is the sex that good? Is the money worth it?" Robin drew in a deep breath to get herself under control and let it out. "Come on, sweetie. We'll never have a better chance. C.D.'s out of town overnight, and we can easily give that thug, Frank Morgan, the slip. I'm all set for us to split. I've got clothes packed for the two of us and plenty of cash. Let's grab Bobby and get the hell out of here. Zander will know what to do."

Milla shook her head violently, fear darkening her eyes. "That's just not possible," she protested. "If I try to leave with him, C.D. really *will* kill me. He'll find me no matter where I go, and I'll be dead meat. And you and Zander, too. Then what happens to Bobby?"

Robin hated the note of panic in Milla's voice. God knew she'd done her best to pull her easily influenced sister away from the charismatic criminal attorney, insisting the marriage would be a disaster. She argued that the rumors about C.D. Ellis's treatment of women couldn't be ignored.

But Milla had stars in her eyes, and C.D., at his most charming, had swept her off her feet, showering her with gifts beyond anything she'd dreamed. Their courtship had been the stuff movies were made of. Milla, so easily influenced, thought she'd landed in a forever fairy tale.

The argument had nearly caused a rift between the sisters, and the wedding took place anyway. Robin had walked down the aisle filled with dread while Milla had floated into what she believed was her perfect marriage. During the entire ceremony, Robin and C.D. were quietly shooting daggers at each other with their eyes.

And in the beginning, it almost seemed to work. Milla was deliriously happy. C.D. gave her whatever she wanted, took her to glamorous places, showered her with attention. Almost a full year passed before the abuse started. It hadn't stopped since, except when Milla was pregnant. Obsessed with producing an heir, C.D. left her alone, unwilling to risk hurting the child.

But three months after Bobby's birth, it began again.

Like most women in her situation, Milla blamed herself and refused to leave, always sure if only she were a better person, if only she didn't upset her husband, if only she knew how to be a better wife. *If only a lot of things*. Her efforts to please the cruel egomaniac tore at Robin's heart.

And despite Milla's insistence that Bobby was the center of his world, the very few times Robin had seen them together, C.D. treated Bobby more like a possession, one who needed to be molded with strict discipline and very little affection. The only positive aspect of the situation was he hadn't yet begun physically abusing the child.

But Robin knew in her gut that one of these days Bobby would do something to displease C.D. and the mask would be off.

So today, Robin had made up her mind that it was time to move. She couldn't leave her sister and nephew in their situation one minute longer. Somehow, she'd have to convince Milla that leaving was her only choice. Once they were away from Seattle, she'd call Zander and he would help them. She knew it.

Cleaning out her bank account, she'd packed what she needed in her car, including some things for Milla, and bought a car seat for Bobby. According to the newspapers, C.D. was out of town overnight on a big case. This might be the one chance for Milla and Bobby to get away.

Somehow, on the phone, she'd convinced Milla to sneak her into the house, but now, her sister was pleading with her to leave before any of the help saw her and reported to C.D.

Robin wanted to scream. "Milla, he's going to kill you one of these days. Or maybe both of you."

"But where could we go that he wouldn't find me?" Milla's voice was tight with her effort to hide her fear. "Not to your place. He'd look there for me first. You know that."

"We're leaving Seattle. Zander will find a safe place for us. I promise you. I've made up my mind. We'll start over together someplace new."

Milla shook her head. "C.D. takes cases all over the country. No matter where I go, he'd have a way to find me. Besides. You have a great life. A terrific job with the McMullen Foundation. A beautiful condo. You can't just up and throw it away."

"Honey, none of that means as much to me as you and Bobby," Robin argued. "Those are things that can be replaced. You have to get away from this man. What happens when he tires of having a child and turns his temper on Bobby?"

"I'll protect him," Milla insisted. "That's why I have to stay."

Robin grabbed her sister's icy hands. "Milla, you can't ignore the reality of this. Come on. I have money for us and everything. All we have to do is get in my car. Now."

Milla yanked her hands back. "Robin, please, let's don't talk about this. Let's just visit for a minute. I have so little time to spend alone with you."

That was certainly true. C.D. monitored every moment of Milla's life. The bodyguard that was never more than inches away from her was supposed to be for her protection. In reality, he was little more than a jailer. Even when she was home, Frank Morgan's presence could be sensed everywhere, even in the air she breathed.

Tonight, Milla pleaded illness to Frank, then locked her bedroom door before Robin arrived. At the moment, he was in the kitchen, reading the paper and drinking coffee with the nanny. But both women knew that he could decide to come check on Milla any time.

At that moment, loud voices drifted up from the front hall and Milla paled.

"Oh, my God. C.D.'s home."

"But the newspaper said he was out of town overnight. I asked you, remember?"

"That's what he told me, too." Milla was shaking. "He lied, just like he always does. Trying to catch me in something. As if I could even breathe without Frank glued to me."

C.D.'s voice came closer. "When was the last time you checked on her?"

"About an hour ago," Frank told him. "She said she didn't feel good and was going to bed."

"And you believed her?" The familiar voice was in the hallway now. "In an hour, she could be gone from here, you stupid fool. And the boy with her." He rattled the doorknob. "Milla? What the hell is the door doing locked?"

"Oh, Jesus. Oh, God." Milla was shaking all over. "Robin, get out on the balcony. Take the stairs going down to the patio." She pushed Robin toward the French doors, shoving her purse into her arms. "Go on right now. He won't have reset the alarm yet."

Robin grabbed her purse and was barely outside before her sister slammed the French doors and locked them. Suddenly, she found herself on the wide balcony. It stretched across the entire back end of the huge house and featured doors that led to assorted bedrooms. The stairways at both ends beckoned, but she'd still have to cross the expanse of lawn and make it out through the gate in the wall to her car in the side street.

She pressed herself to the wall, peering sideways into the room. Sound carried through the glass, and the sheer drapes at the windows were more decorative than covering. Robin froze, tucked away. She could see in but didn't think she'd be spotted. She almost didn't dare to breathe.

"Damn it, Milla, open this door. Now." C.D.'s voice roared into the room.

"Coming." Milla's voice trembled. Through the filmy curtains Robin saw her take a last, fearful look around the room, then hurry toward the door. "Sorry, sorry, sorry."

Robin knew she should get out of there as fast as she could, but she couldn't make her feet move. She heard the panic in each syllable, and a terrible sense of foreboding gripped her.

"Why the hell was this door locked?" C.D. demanded, slamming it open.

"Y-You were out of town, and I'm always afraid Frank will come barging in. I didn't feel well and wanted to be left alone."

Peering in at an angle, Robin saw Milla wringing her hands and backing away from the tall man looming over her. At six foot four, C.D. towered over his petite wife, who barely topped five feet. His lean body vibrated with suppressed energy, and his chiseled face with its ice blue eyes was topped with perfectly barbered dark blond hair. His angelic looks belied the devil that lurked just beneath the surface. The look in his eyes, whenever they met, always terrified her. Not for herself, but for her sister.

"Oh? Is that it? Or did you sneak someone in here when Frank wasn't looking? Some guy, maybe?"

"C.D., you know—"

"I know you're a lying little bitch." His head turned from side to side, scanning the room. "There was someone in here tonight, wasn't there?"

"No, no, I—"

The sound of the blow cut off the rest of the sentence. A crack sounded. On the balcony, Robin flinched as C.D. backhanded Milla across the face, sending her reeling to the floor. Robin flinched as if she'd taken the blow herself. Tears of rage filled her eyes.

She wanted to smash open the doors and hit C.D. with the handiest thing she could find. Anything to show him what pain was like. But she couldn't overpower C.D. and Frank both, and she didn't want to make things worse for Milla.

Worse? What a laugh. How much worse could they be?

Besides, she'd be no help to them if she was beaten to a bloody pulp. Or worse. She'd just have to hope that C.D. would do his usual thing—expend his temper tantrum on Milla, then walk out of the room, leaving her a sobbing mass of flesh. Then Robin would get her and Bobby out of there if she had to drag them by their hair. In the meantime, it took all her willpower to do nothing.

"I said I want the truth." His voice had a dangerous edge of insanity in it. "I don't trust you from here to there. The minute my back is turned, you're in the sack with someone. Admit it." He reached down, pulled Milla up by the front of her sweater, and slammed his fist into her face, then let her fall back to the carpet.

"C.D., please." Milla sounded petrified.

"I haven't had a bad enough day already with an asshole client giving me a hard time? Canceling a meeting with me? I have to put up with this bullshit, too? God knows why I ever married you to begin with, except it was the only way I could get into your pants."

Smack!

The sound of the blow echoed through the glass of the French doors. Robin clenched her fists, willing herself to stay hidden. Standing there and watching Milla take another beating was tearing her apart. If C.D. would just get out of the room, she'd snatch Milla and Bobby and get them the hell out of there.

"Get up," C.D. demanded, his voice thick with rage.

Slowly, Milla pulled herself to her feet. "I-I won't lock the door again. I promise. And there wasn't anyone here. I swear to you. I wouldn't do that. You know that."

"You think I believe a lying bitch like you?"

He slapped her again, and even at that angle Robin could see the blood spurt from her sister's nose, splashing on C.D.'s shirt and jacket. Nausea rose in her throat, and she had to force it back. She started to move toward the French doors, unable to stand another minute of this.

But Milla glanced at the doors, wild-eyed, as if sending Robin a signal.

Don't make it worse. Go away.

She backed away from her husband, using her hand to try and staunch the flow of blood. "Please, C.D."

"Please, C.D.," he mimicked in a nasty tone. "I'll teach you a lesson you won't forget this time. You'll be lucky if I don't throw you out in the street and make sure you never get to see my son again."

"No, no, no," she cried. "Please don't do that. Oh, God, please, please, please."

He raised his hand and put the full force of his body behind the next blow. She cringed as if the blow was aimed at her. Milla flew sideways, cracking her head against the dresser, and slumped to the floor. Robin shoved her fist in her mouth to hold back the scream bubbling up in her throat.

Oh, Milla. Oh, God. I never should have left you alone in there.

"Get up," C.D. ordered. When Milla didn't move, he kicked her ribs, but there was no reaction. "I said get up, damn it. Milla, do you hear me?"

He pushed her head where it had hit the dresser, separating it from the piece of furniture. When she still didn't move, he bent down and pressed his fingers to the pulse at her neck, then at her wrist.

"Christ," he muttered. "God damn it to hell." He stood up and roared, "Frank. Get the hell up here."

Robin was frozen in place, her heart barely beating. Tears burned her eyes. Any minute, she was sure she'd either throw up or pass out. She bit down hard on her knuckles to keep herself from screaming at the top of her lungs. Cold fingers of fear danced on her spine and wrapped themselves around her shaking body.

Should she call nine-one-one? By the time they got here, C.D. could have everything swept under the rug.

Oh, Milla, why didn't you leave with me when I wanted you to?

In a minute, Frank burst into the room.

"What's the matter, boss?" He looked down at Milla. "Oh, oh. What happened?"

"What do you think happened?" He indicated Milla's body. "We have a little problem here. She pushed my buttons once too often, the little slut."

"You need me to call the doc?" Frank asked, strain evident in his voice.

"No, you moron." C.D. sounded as if he wanted to hit Frank, too. "She's dead."

"Jesus, C.D." Frank moved into Robin's line of sight, circling Milla's body as if it were a foreign object from outer space.

At her angle of sight through the curtains, Robin could see C.D. pacing back and forth. "Shit, shit, shit. How the hell did this happen? Goddamn Morelli blows off our meeting today and tells me he can't meet with me until next week. His damn trial's up in two weeks, the schmuck. The pilot had to scurry to get my plane ready to get back here. Then we got stuck in traffic coming home from the airport. And I come home to this. Hell and damnation. This is just the perfect ending to the day."

"So what the hell do we do, boss?"

"Let me think a minute." C.D. was still pacing.

The line of his body, his tone, all said he knew he'd crossed the line this time.

"Boss?" Frank prompted.

"It'll take more than a payoff to sweep this under the rug." C.D.'s voice sounded like sleet on metal. "This is my wife, for Christ's sake. I need a plausible explanation. She can't just disappear like some piece of trash off the street.

Trash? Robin was enraged. He compared sweet Milla to trash? *Oh, God. Milla, I'm so sorry I let this happen. I wish I could have gotten you out of here earlier.*

Tears rolled down her face, and her heart ached so badly she was sure it would actually break. All the two of them had had was each other, and now Milla was gone. Dead by a madman's hands, and she had stood by and let it happen.

Forgive me, Milla. Please, God, forgive me. I'll see this man punished if it's the last thing I do.

C.D. stopped his pacing. "All right, Frank. Get me a bottle of booze. We'll say she was drinking and fell down."

"More than once?" Even Frank's voice was skeptical.

"I can handle it. We'll do our best to get some

12

friendly cops on it and cover it up nice and neat. I can make them believe whatever they want."

"You'd better change your clothes in a hurry before anyone else comes in here." He pointed to C.D.'s chest. "You're a mess."

"You're right." Ellis stripped off everything but his shoes, socks and underwear and tossed the items at Frank, then began grabbing clothes from his closet and dresser. "Here. Get rid of these. But not any place where they can be found."

Robin was shaking so badly she thought her body would fly apart.

Deep breaths. Take deep breaths.

I have to get Bobby away from here. It's the only thing left I can do for Milla. I can save her son.

But she had to do it as fast as she could and then find some place safe. Before C.D. decided to check on him.

Her feet suddenly came unstuck. With an iron will she hadn't known she possessed, she steadied herself and made her way to her nephew's room. It was two doors down, and luckily, the doors to the balcony were unlocked.

If C.D. knew that, he'd beat the nanny black and blue.

Five years old, Bobby slept the sleep of the innocent despite the rage that surrounded him. Robin put her hand over his mouth and shook him lightly.

When his eyes opened, he tried to say something, but she shook her head. "We're going to play a little game, sweetie, okay?"

He stared at her, his eyes wondering.

"We're going to play hide and seek from Daddy. Mommy wants us to. And if we win, we get a big prize, okay? It's real important, Bobby. And you can't make a sound."

He nodded his head.

"I'm going to take my hand off your mouth, but you can only whisper. Got it?" She slipped her hand away from his face.

"Why are we doing this?" he whispered.

"For Mommy. If you want her to get the big prize, you have to be absolutely quiet and do whatever I say. You trust me, don't you, sweetie?"

"Uh huh."

"Okay." She picked him up, amazed at how thin his body was. "Here we go."

She moved quietly through the open doors, along the balcony and down the stairs to the lawn. She waited one moment to make sure no one was out looking for her. Then, taking a deep breath and clutching Bobby tightly, she sprinted across the lawn, thanking her high school track and field coach every step of the way.

"Remember," she kept whispering between panting breaths. "Not a sound, or we won't win the prize."

He bobbed his head, banging it against her shoulder.

She kept to the side where the high hedges grew, all the time waiting for someone to shout out her name or come pounding after her. The gate seemed a million miles away, but at last, she was there. Tightening her grip on Bobby, she pulled it open...and the alarm system went off, loud and screeching. Stealing a quick glance over her shoulder, she saw a figure come out onto the balcony and take the stairs two at a time.

Shit!

Lungs bursting, she raced down the street to where her car was parked. In preparation for stealing Milla and

Bobby away, she'd left her car at her apartment and gotten a rental. C.D. could probably find it with his resources but not before she'd gotten Milla and Bobby out of Seattle and made arrangements. Ducking down on the far side of it, she balanced Bobby on her knee while she dug in her tote for her keys. One pop with the release button and they were inside, seat belts fastened. Her hands were shaking so badly she wasn't sure she could get the key in the ignition.

Then the engine roared to life and she peeled off down the street. Stealing a quick look in her rearview mirror, she saw the man, probably Frank, standing on the sidewalk outside the wall, staring after her.

Please, please, please, don't let him know it's me.

"Are we winning the game, Auntie Robin?" Bobby asked in his high-pitched voice.

"I hope so, sweetie. I sure hope so."

She thanked the good lord she'd withdrawn all that money today. And packed the stuff she had in the car. With her laptop and her iPad, she was all set.

"I'm tired, Auntie Robin." He rubbed his eyes.

"I know you are." She reached one hand in the back and dragged a folded blanket forward, tucking it around him as best she could. "Close your eyes and go to sleep, okay?"

She gripped the wheel so tightly she was afraid her fingers would break. She wanted nothing so much as to pull over to the curb and vomit until her stomach was empty and cry until she had no more tears left. But the safety of a child depended on her. Self-indulgence would have to wait until a later date.

Focusing on the task at hand, she headed down the quiet residential streets toward the edge of the city.

Thirty minutes later, she was on the highway, the lights of Seattle fading behind her. When she found a place to stop for the night, she'd call Zander.

And hope he'd meant it when he said call him any time.

Chapter Two

Frank was panting heavily when he jogged back through the French doors. Only by the slightest chance had he pulled the thin curtains aside and glimpsed someone at the rear gate. He'd taken off at a dead run, but the person had made it to a car and pulled away before he even got to the sidewalk.

"Sorry, C.D." He gulped in a lungful of air. "I was too late. The car was already pulling away, and I couldn't get a plate number." He was still trying to get control of his breathing. "But I think it was a woman."

"Shit." C.D. smacked his hand into his palm. "I'll bet it was that damn busybody sister of hers. I should have given Robin Fletcher some of the same medicine a long time ago. I told her to stay the hell away from Milla." His voice was loud and edgy. "And how the hell did she get in here? Where were you and the stupid nanny?"

"In the kitchen having a cup of coffee, boss," Frank protested. "Jeez. Mrs. Ellis said she was sick and going to bed, and Grace had already put the kid to sleep. Go figure."

"Go figure?" C.D. spat. "I hope to hell, for what I pay you, the two of you weren't playing house on my time." His voice would have chilled hell.

Frank's face turned red. "I know better than that. Boss, what are we going to do?" He looked down at

Milla Ellis's broken body. "We can't just call it in. What if we get the wrong people showing up? Want me just to call some of the cops we take care of and get them to handle it?"

"I'd better check on the kid first. Make sure he didn't wake up through any of this." He looked at Frank. "You take care of the setup with the booze. I'll be right back."

He yanked open the door and headed down the hall with long, angry strides, already forming the story of his wife's alcoholism in his head. He nearly bowled over Grace, the nanny, who was headed in his direction, a distraught look on her face.

"Oh, Mr. Ellis." Her face was white, and her lips trembled.

Now what?

"What is it, Grace? I'm just on my way to see my son. We've had an…incident here tonight."

"That's just it," she wailed, her fear of C.D.'s legendary temper in every line of her body. "He's not in his room."

"What the hell do you mean? Who's not in his room?"

"Bobby, sir." She was shaking with fear. "I can't find him."

Ellis glared at her. "I thought you put him to bed ages ago."

"I did, I did. I just went to check on him and…the room's empty."

C.D. stormed into the nursery and stopped short at the sight of the empty bed, covers thrown back. The doors to the balcony were standing open.

"I thought I told you to lock these doors at all times,"

he raged, yanking them shut. "Someone's been in here. Damn you."

Grace stood at the foot of the bed, twisting her hands together.

Moving his eyes back and forth from the nanny to the empty bed, in that split instant, C.D. Ellis made a decision. Luck, or its counterpart, had handed him not only a way out of this problem but also a way to take care of another one. This would play even better than a drunken wife.

He took Grace's arm, his attitude suddenly grave. "You'd better come into the master bedroom. We've had an intruder in the house. Now I know why. I was just about to call the police. It's bad, Grace. Very bad. Mrs. Ellis was attacked."

Grace stumbled when she saw Milla's body on the floor. "Oh, my God." Her hand went to her mouth. "Don't we need to call the doctor, too?"

Making his voice as distressed as possible, C.D. shook his head. "She's dead, Grace. I had to get Frank to use my key to open the door to the room. It was locked. It appears she'd been drinking again. She might have seen someone on the balcony and stumbled out to see who it was. That's probably when they killed her."

Grace's eyes filled with tears. She twisted her trembling hands together. "It can't have been too long ago." She stole a glance at Frank.

"It had to be quite a while," C. D, lied, moving the woman away from Milla's body. "The blood is dried. I just walked in and found her like this."

He let out a long breath and forked his fingers through his hair again, hoping he looked appropriately upset. Which he was, with his son missing. His heir. The child who would carry on the Ellis name.

"Oh, my God," Grace said again, her face a pasty white. "This is terrible. I'm sorry. I'm so sorry. Time just got away from me." Her eyes were terrified as she looked at her boss.

"How the hell did someone get past you and Frank? And the alarm system?"

Grace kept looking at Frank again, who was avoiding her eyes.

"We need to call the police," C.D. told the frightened woman. "Don't touch anything in here. They'll want to dust for fingerprints and look for any other traces that might give them a lead."

"Poor Mrs. Ellis," Grace wailed. "She must have been fighting them for Bobby."

"Yes." C.D. gritted his teeth. "That's probably what happened. Go downstairs in the kitchen now and wait for me while I make the calls. Fix yourself a cup of tea."

She scurried out of the room without looking at him and almost ran down the stairs.

C.D. was sure in his gut that Robin Fletcher, that nosy, interfering bitch, had been in the room with his wife tonight. She had to have been hiding on the balcony. If she left by the door, Frank would have seen her. He'd bet money that she saw what happened to her sister and snuck Bobby out of the house.

Well, that wasn't acceptable. But she had unwittingly handed him the perfect cover for Milla's death and a way to get rid of her at the same time.

"This changes everything," C.D. told Frank. "Forget about the bottle of booze. I have a better story. But first, I have some things for you to do before the police get here."

The first fingers of morning light were wiping away the blackness of the night by the time the Crime Scene Unit left. Captain Harlan Davis, head of homicide and in charge of the team investigating the crime, left a man and some telephone monitoring equipment set up in the dining room.

"In case they put in a ransom call," he explained to Ellis. "You're a very wealthy man, which makes your son a tempting target."

Shit.

He'd refused to let Davis call in the FBI for the moment, adamantly arguing against it.

"Let's see if whoever it is makes contact," he insisted. "Maybe we can get Bobby back right away and unharmed."

Davis was not happy with him. "The sooner we call in the troops, the faster we'll resolve this," he argued. "How long did you say it was before you discovered your wife dead and the boy missing?"

"The nanny put him to bed around seven. I got home about nine o'clock and found Milla." He looked away. "The nanny was just checking on Bobby and discovered him missing."

"So this happened sometime during that two-hour span," Davis mused. "And you said the blood around the body had already dried when you found her. Right?"

C.D. nodded. "That's correct."

"Did you try to revive her at all? Check for a pulse?"

C.D. shook his head. "I could tell right away she was dead. I've seen enough dead bodies, unfortunately."

He watched a strange look flit across Davis's face. Then it was gone as suddenly as it had appeared.

What's that all about?

"And you're still adamant about not calling in the feds?"

"Yes. Something is going on here, and I don't want the FBI screwing it up."

"I can't see that having them here would hurt anything," Davis protested.

In point of fact, Ellis wanted more ammunition in case the FBI arrived on the scene. Enough to point to his miserable sister-in-law. Then let Robin Fletcher see if she could hide. He'd have his own men shadowing the feds and hopefully get to her first.

He thought he'd done a masterful job of playing the bereaved husband and distraught father. The last was actually true. The one positive thing Milla had done was produce an heir for him, even if the child was often a pain in the ass to handle. Getting rid of Milla would have taken care of that, an act he was already planning. Just a little…differently.

Frank had stashed the bloody clothes in the trunk of his car. Later, when he could leave without causing comment, he'd take them someplace and destroy them.

The men who came to his house had not been his first choice to handle things. Frank had called their friends on the force, but because the case would be so high profile, an elite homicide team now had ownership of it. For Ellis, this meant watching every word and crossing every T. He knew that, regardless of the fact his son was missing, in a case like this, police always looked at the spouse first as the primary suspect.

C.D. was impatient for everyone to leave, but Captain Davis continued to question him at length. He took him through it again and again, but C.D. had coached enough witnesses to know how to keep his story straight without sounding rehearsed. Did he have any enemies? they asked. Were they stupid? Of course he did. Every client he hadn't defended successfully. And maybe even the cops who resented him, he'd added. That one didn't sit too well, but he thought, what the hell. Don't leave anyone out.

What about other people? Sure. People in his profession always had enemies.

Family members? Well…With just the right note of reluctance, he mentioned that his sister-in-law disapproved of the marriage and was, in fact, insanely jealous of Milla and their child.

"Do you think she'd kill her own sister and take the boy?" Davis wanted to know. "That seems a little extreme."

C.D. shrugged eloquently but said nothing. Let them find Robin's fingerprints and draw their own conclusions. Especially if, as he surmised, she had already hauled ass out of town.

"The wire to the alarm system was cut," Davis pointed out.

I know that. I had Frank take care of it.

"She's not a stupid woman," C.D. told him. "If she was planning this, she'd figure out how to disable the alarm. The box is hidden but not impossible to get to. And she could easily sneak up the back stairs to the balcony."

"Would your wife have opened the doors for her if, as you say, there was bad blood between them?"

C.D. drywashed his face. "I don't think Milla had a clue how her sister felt. So yes, if Robin showed up without warning, Milla would let her in. And that's the only way she'd be able to get into this house. Since I learned the depth of her hatred for Milla, I've left orders with the staff not to admit her."

Frank and Grace also spent hours answering questions, but Frank knew how to play the "I know nothing" card very well. And Grace was so hysterical no one could get a coherent sentence out of her.

"You won't get anything out of her tonight," he told Davis as he sent the woman to bed.

He left the cop still setting up his phone traps and other paraphernalia and took Frank into the den.

"I'll have limited ability to do anything here as long as these people are crawling all over the place," he told him. "They'll be watching me like a hawk. But no one will miss you if you're gone. Get some help and toss Robin Fletcher's condo. See if she's actually left town, and look for anything that might tell you where she'd go."

"You're sure it's her, C.D.?"

"Oh, hell, yes. The more I think about it, the more I'm convinced Milla sneaked her in here, thinking I was away. Then she had to get rid of her quickly, so I'm sure she shoved her out onto the balcony. Too damn fucking bad she had to see that unfortunate scene in the bedroom from wherever she was. But she's such a do-gooder. I know she grabbed Bobby to get him away from here." His lips thinned. "Bitch."

"Okay. I'll get Kenny to go with me."

"Get one of those cops we support so grandly to pull up her license plate number and send out the word. I'd do it, but I don't want to take the chance of being overheard here. If I wait until I can get to my office, she'll have too big a head start."

"Which direction do you think she'd take?" Frank

asked.

"My guess is she'll stay on the Interstate through Oregon because it's the fastest way to travel. Then she'll cut over somewhere to the east. She won't want to chance staying anywhere on the west coast. We have to find her before she goes to ground. Put the word out to everyone."

"And then what?"

C.D. looked at him with eyes like ice chips. "Kill her ass and take the boy. What else?"

Chapter Three

Taking the interstate highway might have been easier on her, but Robin was sure that was the first route C.D. would check. Instead, she cut east immediately into Idaho, taking highways but not the Interstate, and began looking for a motel. She needed one bland and not too obvious. She wasn't worried about her car. She'd had the foresight to get a rental before heading to her sister's, and she figured it would take C.D. a while to think about that. He had no reason to, at the moment, and she hoped her phone call she planned to make would eliminate the danger.

Robin had only a vague idea of how long they'd been driving as they passed town after town, but it felt as if she'd been doing it forever. Her eyes were gritty from lack of sleep, and her muscles rigid with tension. It didn't help that she was constantly watching for some car to run her off the road.

She'd been lucky enough to find a couple of drive-throughs where she fueled up with coffee. Caffeine raced through her system like a wild horse, revving her up and making her edgy, but she had to keep going. She needed to find a place to stop soon and grab some sleep, but before that, she'd make her phone call.

She slid a glance over her shoulder at Bobby, wrapped in a blanket and buckled into his car seat. What a lucky thing he was sleeping so heavily. Still, she knew they needed to find a bed pretty soon. And food. Starvation wouldn't be a pretty way to die.

By the time they reached Kellogg, Idaho, she was more than ready to stop. She pulled gratefully into a motel whose sign blinked 'Vacancy' in big red letters. It was the most welcoming site Robin had seen in a long time.

Registering was a problem since she couldn't use her ID, but the old man behind the counter apparently had a soft spot for single mothers in the middle of the night. Nervously, she left Bobby in the car, keeping one eye on the parking lot. She was terrified that, any moment, she'd hear the screeching of brakes and C.D. would leap out of his car. At last, they were in their room at the back of the motel, well hidden from the street. She toted in her duffel bag and laptop, then tucked the little boy into bed.

After that, she treated herself to a shower. Tired as she was, she still needed to wash away the strain of driving nearly three hundred miles at night. All she wanted was to wash the fatigue from her muscles before she climbed into bed. But as the hot spray beat down on her physically and emotionally exhausted body, her control disintegrated and tears began to cascade down her cheeks. She was thankful that the drumming of the water against the tiles drowned out the huge gulping sobs that wracked her body, so Bobby couldn't hear.

She cried as she had never cried before in her life, tears of despair and grief. And self-condemnation that she hadn't been able to do anything to save her sister. She didn't think that particular guilt would ever leave her.

Milla! Oh, Milla! How did I let this happen to you?

The water ran cold before the last shudder died from her body. She drew in a long breath and blew it out slowly. Her heart ached unbearably, but she had a responsibility now. A mission, and she would not fail, no matter what. Keep Bobby safe and away from C.D. Create a whole new life for the two of them. This would be her tribute to her sister.

She dried her hair as best she could with the towel and dug clean panties and a long T-shirt out of the duffel bag. After double checking that all the locks were set on the door and pushing a heavy chair in front of it, just in case.

Then she pulled out her phone and scrolled for a number she hadn't used in a long time. She only hoped it still worked. And that he'd listen to her. When she wouldn't leave and go with him to San Antonio, they hadn't parted on the best of terms. It was very late, but she took a chance, anyway. She didn't want to wait until morning.

He answered on the third ring. "Zander Craig."

The deep, slightly gravelly voice was like a match to the fire of stored memories. At once, the images of the tall, athletic man with thick black hair and ebony eyes popped into her brain.

"Zander? It's me. Robin Davis. You, um, said to call you if I ever needed anything."

"Robin?" Shock edged his voice. "What's up? What do you need? It's the middle of the night, so it must be pretty important."

That was Zander. No bitching because of the hour. No criticism for not having called him all these months. Just what did she need? She hoped that was an omen.

"I need help. I know I have no right to call at this

28

hour and—"

"Forget that. You wouldn't be calling me at this hour if you didn't need help. What can I do?"

The tension eased slightly from her body. After all these months, he was ready to do whatever she needed. At least, she hoped he was. Letting out a breath, she gave him the abbreviated version of her situation, leaving out the fact that she saw C.D. kill her sister. Zander would only make her go to the police. She was relieved that he listened carefully, not interrupting her.

"Milla is dead, C.D. killed her, and I have Bobby. I'm afraid C.D. is already on my tail. I need someplace for Bobby and me to hide. Right away before he gets all his thugs fully mobilized. Someplace where C.D. won't even think to look for us. I know I have no right to ask, but can you help us?"

There was a slight pause, and she gripped the phone harder as she waited for his response.

"I can do that," he said at last. "You can always ask me for help. I hope you know that. Did you report your sister's death before you left?"

"No. I just got the hell out of there. I was afraid I might be next if I tried to. Besides, C.D. has so much influence, he can manipulate the situation any way he wants."

"Okay, I'll check quietly and see if the word is out yet and if your name is floated with it anywhere. We'll discuss that later. Right now, the goal is to keep you and Bobby safe." He paused. "The best thing for now is to bring you to San Antonio."

Guardian Security, the agency Zander was with now, was headquartered in San Antonio, and Zander obviously had his base of operation there now, also.

"San Antonio? How will we get there? It's a long drive."

"Right. That's out. Besides, you said your car is a rental. C.D. can trace it with his connections. Hold on a sec."

She closed her eyes and prayed while she waited.

"Okay, take down these directions to a small airport about fifty miles from where you are. Luckily, we have an agent working a case there. He'll be waiting for you at the FBO—Fixed Base Operations Building. Stay with him until I get there."

"It's just as long a drive for you."

His laugh was low. "Ah, but Guardian has a plane, and I now have my license. See you shortly."

Zander had a pilot's license? Well, he'd mentioned wanting one, and she was doubly glad it had happened.

Minutes later, she had directions to the airport where someone would be waiting for her.

As tired as she was, she couldn't help thinking about her closest friend, Meg Riley, the person she shared everything with. Meg would be hysterical with worry, but she'd have an inkling of what was going on as soon as the story hit the media. Not even dynamite would break information loose from her.

Then there was Sawyer McMullen, director of his family's mammoth foundation and the kind of boss people killed to work for. Her conscience weighed heavily over just walking out this way.

But superimposed over all the images clashing in her brain was the one of Milla's bloody, broken body. And the knowledge she represented Bobby's only safe harbor. No way was she going to let C.D. get his hands on Bobby. Milla had given her life to protect him. Robin wasn't going to let that sacrifice go to waste.

She repacked the few things she'd taken out of the suitcase and shook Bobby awake.

"Wake up, sport. We're going for another ride."

Bobby rubbed his eyes and grumbled, "But I just went to sleep."

"You can sleep on the way." She grinned at him. "We're going for a plane ride."

"Yeah?" His eyes widened at that. "Is Mommy coming too? You said we were playing a game."

Her heart nearly broke at that.

Mommy. Right. Robin was on the run, and Mommy was dead. Very dead. And she couldn't tell a soul she'd witnessed a murder. C.D. would have her eliminated before she could tell her story.

"Where are we going, Aunt Robin?"

"On an adventure, sport. Is that okay?" She smoothed his hair back from his forehead. "We're playing road trip and hiding from everyone."

"But what about Mommy?" His lower lip began to tremble. "Why isn't she with us? When can I see her?"

"Mommy wants us to do this, okay?"

Two fat tears trailed down each of his cheeks. "Is it because of Daddy?"

Oh, dear lord. Does he know what's going on?

"What do you mean, sweetheart?" She stroked his shoulder, feeling the thinness of his body beneath the pajama material.

He bit his lip. Hard. And dropped his eyes.

"Bobby? Whatever it is, you can tell me." She kissed away his tears. "Honest. You know your mommy and I tell each other everything."

He buried his face against her shoulder. "Did she tell

you he hurts her sometimes? She thinks I don't know, but he's very mean to her."

Robin's heart pinched. How dreadful that this child, not quite five, should even know about such things.

"How do you know that?" she asked.

"Sometimes, when they think I'm asleep, I hear him yell at her, and she screams." He sniffled. "And the next day, she cries all the time, and she's got places where she hurts. And bruises like when I fell down the stairs."

Robin took the thin shoulders and pulled Bobby slightly away from her. "I want you to tell me something. Did your dad ever hurt you in any way? Tell me the truth, Bobby."

He shook his head. "No. Not like that. But…"

Oh, God. Please don't let me think what I'm thinking.

"But what, sweetie?"

"He…he tells me he loves me. But I don't think he really does. He yells at me a lot when Mommy doesn't know." He ducked his head again, hiding it against her shoulder. "I'm afraid of him, Aunt Robin. And I hate the way he hurts Mommy."

"Oh, sweetheart." She pulled him in for another quick hug. "Okay, then. Yes. Your mommy wants us to go on this road trip. Kind of like playing hide and seek, got it? We're going to hide from your daddy. Would you like that?"

Please like it, Bobby. Please go along with the game.

He sniffled again and rubbed the heel of his hand against his eyes. "But will Mommy come to wherever we are?" When she didn't answer, two fat tears rolled down his cheeks. "At least he can't hurt her anymore."

"Right now, we need to get going to our plane ride."

When they were ready, she pulled the curtain back and checked the motel's back parking lot very carefully. She'd be surprised if someone was waiting for her, though. If C.D.'s men had caught up to her by now, they'd have no qualms about breaking down the door to get to her and Bobby. Finally, when nothing rang any alarm bells—although how the hell she'd know she wasn't sure—she opened the door. Grabbing her laptop and duffel with one hand and hoisting Bobby up in her other arm, she raced for the car.

****

Zander thought he'd done a good job at concealing his shock when he heard Robin's voice. He was sure he'd never see her again, although he had been working on a plan in his mind. How the hell had she gotten herself into trouble that would require his special skills? He was aware from his time in Seattle of her bother-in-law's aggressive personality, but he never thought the man would resort to murder. How the hell had it even happened?

He'd get the details from Robin and then pull a protective curtain around both of them. He could talk to the partners about giving him some time off the books so he could devote himself full time to Robin and Bobby. He'd also see if Guardian Security could take this on "behind the curtain," so to speak and dig up the details. He had a good working relationship with the police, but he needed all the information on this. Robin and Bobby would be under his protective custody until this thing came to a head.

Maybe he should meet with the Seattle detectives.

No, don't call attention to yourself.

He'd spend his time with Robin and Bobby and get the people at Guardian to dig up everything they could. And when her nerves had settled, he hoped to restore the intimacy they'd shared, because that was what he really wanted—a tight relationship that looked like a family.

Meanwhile, he needed to talk to Reno or Nick about the situation.

****

On the drive, she tried to watch in her mirror for any car that might be following her, but nothing seemed out of the ordinary. Again, she wondered how she would even know.

I'm not very good at this game, but I better learn fast.

She made one quick stop at a big box store to pick up a few things for Bobby, then they were on the road again. She joked with him and teased him to keep his mind occupied and also to prevent him from asking any questions about his mother. Then, thankfully, he dozed off and slept for the last thirty minutes of the drive.

The airport was small, with a few planes at tie-downs and one hanger. And a small concrete building that served as the FBO. As soon as she pulled into a parking space, a man came out holding a sign that said "Zander sent me."

She had to laugh.

"He wanted you to feel safe," the man told her. "Greg Daniels. Come on, let's get you two inside. Zander will be here shortly."

The building had some basic supplies, so they found a juice box and crackers for Bobby and coffee for her. Greg chatted with her in a way tailored to help her relax, which was almost impossible, and an hour later, they heard the sound of a plane approaching.

"Hold on," Greg told her. "Let me make sure it's Zander."

She waited tensely until the plane had landed, and shortly, Greg walked in with a familiar person she'd never been so glad to see. The lean but muscular body, the thick black hair, the midnight blue eyes and the tiny scar on his chin were so familiar, she felt her nerves start to settle at once. He'd shown up for her just like that, and all the feelings she'd buried toward him came surging back. She had no idea how he felt except he'd answered her plea for help without question. Maybe this was a second chance for them. Throwing caution and history to the wind, she leaped into his arms and hugged him tightly. Thankfully, his arms closed around her and held her tight for a moment to his hard, warm body.

"Whoa! I guess it must be pretty desperate here."

She took a step back, suddenly embarrassed. "Is it okay that I called you?"

"I wouldn't have it any other way." He looked down at Bobby, who had plastered himself to Robin's side. "And this must be Bobby. Ready for an airplane ride, sport?"

He clutched Robin tighter but nodded his head.

"Okay, then. Greg, can you gas me up and we'll be out of your hair?"

"Not a problem. Let's do it."

The plane was a tricked-out Beechcraft Bonanza, but of course, Guardian would go first class. Reno Sullivan and Nick Vanetta had turned the whole operation into a first-class organization with clients now all over the world.

They settled Bobby in the rear seat with a pillow and

a blanket and shortly took off and pulled away from the little airport.

"So you're taking me to San Antonio?" she asked when they were in the air.

"Safest place. C.D. won't think to look for you there. Even if he knew about me, he has no idea I now work for Guardian."

"But where will we stay? I can't afford any place for long. I brought cash with me, but I don't want to use credit cards that he can trace."

"Please." He slid a quick glance over at her. "No motels for you, kiddo. You'll stay with me. I have a nice safe condo. I know, I know. All the partners have houses in Northwest San Antonio except Nick who lives on a ranch, but I've never been a house person. It even has a guest suite where you and Bobby can be comfortable and have privacy while I work on your…situation."

"Zander, I—"

He gave her hand a quick squeeze.

"Don't thank me. I'm happy to do this."

His touch brought back familiar memories, and everything else aside, she gave huge thanks for this man next to her. It seemed she hadn't killed their relationship after all. But that was for later. Right now, her priority was getting Bobby settled and figuring out what to do next.

Chapter Four

"What do you mean there's no trace of them?"

C.D. Ellis paced back and forth on his patio, his cell phone clamped to his ear. Rage simmered beneath his granite exterior, flashing like the fires of hell in his eyes.

"Listen, C.D," Frank was saying at the other end of the call. "We took that condo apart to the walls, but we couldn't find a damn thing. She doesn't even have an address book."

"Hell. She probably keeps it all on her phone, you dimwit." *Shit.* He should have thought of that himself. His mind wasn't functioning clearly, and he needed to get a grip on himself. Anger blunted everything. "All right. Look for mail, bills, correspondence. Anything like that."

Everyone has some kind of personal life. There's something hidden there somewhere.

"We'll keep going, but I'm not optimistic. I just want you to know that. It looks like she cleared away or destroyed anything personal that might give us a direction to look."

"That's not what I want to hear," C.D. ground out. "Get me something, anything, because she's got a good head start on us. Jesus, Frank. We can find a needle in a haystack, and we can't find one woman and a little boy?"

"You want me to check out the neighbors?"

C.D. shook his head, even though he knew Frank

couldn't see him. "No. Not yet." *Not until the police find her fingerprints here and I point them in her direction.* "Tomorrow you can contact her office. Ask for her and see what they say. Did you call our cop friends and put a trace on her car?"

"Just like you said. Nothing there yet, either."

"Damn. Where the hell could she have disappeared to?"

"What about relatives?"

"Their parents are dead so that's not a possibility. And Milla never mentioned any other relatives." *As if I even cared.* "Get back to it and call me again later."

He had barely disconnected the call when another one came through, this one from his computer expert. The man was not shy about skirting the law, and C.D. had used him many times when preparing cases.

"I've got something for you," were his first words.

"Thank God at least someone does." C.D. blew out a breath.

"Her account shows she made a huge withdrawal yesterday. Just about cleaned it out. That help you at all?"

"Only that it tells me she had some kind of plan she was hatching." He thought for a moment. "As soon as the police pick up on her, they'll check it out, too. It will at least show some kind of premeditation. The problem is, she can go to ground anywhere now and stay hidden."

"But not forever," the man reminded him. "Sooner or later, she'll need some income."

"You keep monitoring everything. Check every database that might give us a hit. I want to know where that damned woman is, and I want to know now."

"I'm on it, C.D. Don't worry."

"Don't worry. Yeah, right."

He'd barely finished with that call when one of the cops monitoring the phone called to him from the open doors.

"Captain Davis and another man are here to see you, sir. They're waiting in the living room."

C.D. turned his phone off and stuck it in his pocket. No way did he want the calls he expected to pop up while he was talking to the police. He ran his fingers through his hair again, carefully adjusted his face into a distressed look, and went to find the captain and whoever was with him.

"This is Mac Fontaine," Davis told him, introducing the man next to him. "He'll actually be handling the details of the case and coordinating with the FBI."

C.D. hated the man on sight. Beneath the conservative sports jacket and tie was a lean, muscular body with the alertness of a jungle cat. The hard, granite planes of his face indicated a man who had seen a lot of life and didn't let much stand in the way of whatever his mission was.

A cop's cop, C.D. thought instantly. *A bulldog. He'll be impossible to manipulate.*

Oh, come on, C.D. Think of it as playacting before a jury. You've sold them the Brooklyn Bridge before. You can make it work with this man.

"The Crime Scene Unit reported in," Davis told him. "They left me with both answers and questions."

"All I want to know is have you gotten any leads on my son?" C.D. demanded. "I'm getting tired of people just sitting around and nothing happening. I want to see some results."

"Why don't you have a seat, Mr. Ellis," Fontaine

said, his voice as hard as his looks. "I can assure you nobody's just sitting around. Believe me. I wouldn't be here if we were. But we've come up with something I think we need to discuss."

"I don't need to sit down." He shoved his hands in his pockets, trading Fontaine glare for glare. "I want answers, and I can hear them better standing up."

"Fine." Fontaine gave him a flat look. *Davis is letting him take the lead. I don't think I like that.*

"Does your sister-in-law, Robin Fletcher, spend a lot of time here?" Fontaine asked. "From what I've learned, you and she weren't exactly on the best of terms."

Okay. At least he's caught it. Here it comes. Handle it right, and you're home free.

"No. As a matter of fact, I felt she was a bad influence on my wife. Why?" He clenched his fists in his pockets to control his excitement, waiting for the answer.

"We processed all the fingerprints in your bedroom and the boy's. When we ran them through AFIS, we found hers all over both places." Fontaine was still giving him the same look. "When was she here last?"

C.D. knew AFIS was the Automated Fingerprint Information System. Every police department had access to it. Robin had been fingerprinted as part of the security process when she went to work for the foundation. He could barely keep from grinning and clapping his hands. This was working out better than he expected.

"I'd say at least six months ago. Certainly long enough for the maid to have dusted and removed any prints she left, if that's what you want to know." He forced a look of shock on his face. "Why? Do you think she had anything to do with this?"

"You tell me."

"How did she feel about not seeing her sister?" Davis broke in. "And her nephew?"

Careful, careful, careful.

"I know she hated me and was jealous of Milla." He looked down at his feet, then back up at the two men. "She has no one special in her life that I know of. Certainly no husband or children. No family of her own. She could have wanted Bobby for herself."

"Enough to kill her sister?" Davis's voice held just a touch of skepticism.

"Maybe." Ellis shifted his gaze away from them, focusing on a spot on the wall, unwilling to let them see the excitement he was sure was reflected in his eyes. "Her temper and jealousy were among the reasons I didn't want Milla to have anything to do with her."

"Well, we've spoken to everyone in the house and your neighbors on both sides," Davis said. "No one spotted whoever it was that killed your wife and took your son."

Right. I told Frank to keep his mouth shut. I don't want it to look like I'm pointing fingers. Let them draw their own conclusions.

"We also discovered the alarm was cut," Fontaine pointed out. "Would your sister-in-law be the kind to do something like that? And how would she know you weren't home?"

"The newspaper ran an article about the new case I'm handling. It mentioned that I'd be out of town for a day or two." C.D. looked back at the men, his attention on Mac, picturing him as the one doubting juror he had to convince. He waved a hand impatiently. "I'm assuming she saw that as her big chance. But you're the cops, not me. Damn it, I want my son back and my wife's

41

murderer brought to justice."

"And that will happen, Mr. Ellis," Davis assured him. "We've got a BOLO out for Robin Fletcher's car— Be On the Look Out. She didn't show up for work today or call in, so that doesn't look too good for her. The foundation director also gave us the name of a close friend and a man she'd brought to a couple of functions."

C.D. tried to conceal his excitement at the information. A direction in which he could point Frank. He'd have to find someplace to make a call in private.

"But we don't want to focus just on her," Fontaine told him. "We need to cover all bases."

"How sure are you that this isn't just someone you've crossed paths with who could be carrying a grudge against you?" Davis asked in his gravelly voice. "One strong enough to do something like this. You've dealt with a lot of people who don't think the law's for them."

"I'm a highly respected criminal defense lawyer, Captain." C.D. worked to get just the right note of indignation in his voice. "My clients have usually been wronged by the law, not the other way around."

"Save the rhetoric for another time, Mr. Ellis." Fontaine's voice was hard and uninflected. "Right now, finding your wife's killer and the kidnapper of your son are the top priorities. I know you don't want us to call in the FBI right away, but I think that's a mistake. While the murder is in our jurisdiction, kidnapping is theirs. I can't sit on this forever."

"You're right." Instant contrition. A sad look. "I was just hoping we could bring this thing to a quick conclusion. But that was before you found all the fingerprints."

"Pretty strong evidence," Davis said in a mild voice.

"Yes, it is. If the FBI can help you find Robin Fletcher and my son, then have at it. And right away." C.D. looked down at his feet. "If she's the one who did this—and I'm more and more convinced that she is—I want everyone in the country looking for her."

He took a steadying breath, putting on what his secretary called his jury face. "God knows what harm she'll do to my son if you don't find her soon."

That's it. Let him see you're upset. Anxious. Frightened, even.

"We're still checking out that list of former clients you gave us," Fontaine reiterated. "As well as their associates. You know we can't just ignore that."

C.D. lifted his eyes to glare at the man. "You know what you have to do. But if one of them did this, don't you think we'd have heard from them by now? What would be the use in committing this crime if they didn't let me know they were the ones who did it? Demand a ransom? We haven't even gotten a call." He shook his head. "No, the more I think about it, the more I'm convinced it's Robin. I want her charged with kidnapping and hunted down." It wasn't hard to set his face in lines of anger. "I want my son back."

"My men are still checking out her condo looking for clues," Davis told him. "I'll let you know what they find, if anything. I'm also getting a warrant for her bank records. Where will you be if I need you?"

"Right here. Where else would I be? You think I can work at a time like this?"

"Fine. I'll get back to you."

Yeah. You do that, asshole. Meanwhile, I'll do whatever I have to in order to find that bitch and get my son back. And make that woman sorry she ever stuck her nose in my business.

****

"I think we got more out of that than Ellis intended us to," Mac Fontaine commented. He was steering the unmarked police car through traffic, Captain Davis sitting quietly beside him lost in his own thoughts.

"I have to agree with you." He roused himself. "He puts on a good act, but then he's been doing that in the courtroom for years."

"I know we don't have the evidence," Fontaine went on, "but I'd bet my paycheck for the rest of the year that Ellis is guilty as sin. I looked at the autopsy report. Milla Ellis had a lot of old bruises and fractures. You know what that means."

David nodded. "Abuse. And constant."

"I've heard Ellis has a vicious temper that he has to work to keep under control. It wouldn't surprise me at all if something set him off and he beat her to death."

Mac maneuvered around a large truck backing into a driveway. "Do we think the sister was a witness and grabbed the kid to get him out of there?"

"With no ransom and no notes, that makes the most sense to me." He blew out a breath of frustration. "That asshole lawyer isn't quite as smart as he thinks he is, trying to convince us a woman not much bigger than the victim could beat her sister to death like that. I'd like nothing better than to pull the rug out from under him. Still, we have to follow protocol."

"I'll call Joel Stetler at the local FBI office as soon as we're back at the station," Mac told him. "And I guess we'll get the U.S. Marshal's service to put Robin Fletcher on their 'catch' list."

The U.S. Marshal's office, among other things, was responsible for tracking and bringing in fugitives from justice. Both men knew they were opening a big can of worms here, but there weren't a lot of options.

"I hate doing it, but she'll be a lot safer if the Marshals grab her rather than one of Ellis's men. He may very well kill her if he finds her first."

"I'll get things started.

****

Dawn was just lighting up the sky when Zander landed the plane at a small, private airport. Pulling into a hangar, he cut the engines and helped Robin and Bobby from the plane. The little boy mumbled and stirred in his sleep, but then automatically wound his arms around Zander's neck. In seconds, they were beside a black SUV and Zander was arranging him on the back seat.

At the jostling, he opened his eyes, panic flashing across his face until his gaze landed on Robin.

"It's okay, kiddo," she told him. "Zander is taking care of us."

"Will he hide us from my dad?"

She nodded, her heart breaking at the obvious fear of his father. "That's the plan."

Then they were rolling out of the airport and down the Interstate.

"You have no idea how much I appreciate this." Robin glanced over at Zander. "I wasn't sure if when I called you'd—"

"I'm always here for you, Robin," he cut in. "No matter what happened between us, that doesn't change." He looked as if he wanted to say something else but stopped himself. Only the tic of a muscle in his jaw indicated the situation between them.

"Well, thank you. I had no idea where else to turn."

She glanced over her shoulder at Bobby, now wide awake in the back seat, fear plainly stamped on his face. She couldn't imagine what was going through his mind. How would he take to all of this? What explanation could she give him about his mother? What reason could she give for never seeing her again that wouldn't completely traumatize him?

Briefly, she wondered what would happen with her condo and what her bosses at the McMullen foundation were thinking. And her friends. Well, thank the lord, none of them knew about Zander, and the condo could rot for all she cared. She had more important things on her list.

Her stomach knotted as she looked into the black hole of the future. Could Zander really find proof of what C.D. had done? More importantly, how far would he be willing to go to help her? And at some point, they had to face the elephant in the room—the way she'd broken things off with him.

She swallowed hard against the nausea that rose in her throat.

Just take it one hour at a time. At least you know Zander will do his best to keep you safe. But could he protect her from C.D. and his thugs? Would the agency he worked for allow him to?

"I smell your brain burning," Zander teased. "We'll talk. Okay? Everything else aside, I am not about to let anything happen to you or that little guy in the back seat."

"But—"

"You reached out to me because you know I can help you. Let me do that. But first, let's get you settled."

They rode in silence, then Zander finally pulled off the highway and eventually into the underground garage of a large building.

"My condo is here," he told her. "There's a guard twenty-four/seven, and I have state of the art security. You'll be safe here. Come on, Let's get you inside."

Chapter Five

Less than twenty-four hours later, the manhunt was on in full force, and C.D. Ellis had a hard time concealing his excitement. Even though Captain Davis and Mac Fontaine still insisted they couldn't ignore other possibilities, the search, for the moment, was focused on Robin Fletcher. Her picture was on the front page of every major newspaper, and television channels from local stations to national news had the story front and center.

He was a little concerned that they'd sicced the Marshals on her. He couldn't really afford to have anyone but his men grab her. But they could follow the leads and, if they were lucky, get to her before anyone from any law enforcement agency got their hands on her.

At the urging of the police, C.D. agreed to go on camera and make a plea for the return of his son. Frank, who was now at his side all the time, told him it was an award-winning performance.

He wanted the police to release the body so he could stage the funeral. His secretary had taken the reins that morning and run with it, ready to push the buttons as soon as it was possible. Neither he nor Milla were churchgoers, but Melanie insisted they needed a church service. Somehow, she managed to tentatively schedule one at the church she and her husband attended, although it meant an endless hour with the minister making sure his grief didn't slip for a moment.

Melanie also put city dignitaries and ranking judges on notice, selecting those she wanted to speak at the service and the attendance read like a slice of a national Who's Who. Even people who hated C.D.'s guts would show up, afraid of the backlash if they didn't.

Meanwhile, he was locked up at home, the picture of the angry, grieving husband, demanding answers and results. Acting for all the world like a man who had lost the love of his life. All those years of posturing in the courtroom, playing a part, and training witnesses paid off in spades. Frank Morgan and Melanie Jacobs fielded all calls. People called the house to express their dismay, but it was all superficial. One thing was abundantly clear, though, from the tone of the conversations. C.D. had many acquaintances but apparently no friends.

Well, fuck them all. He didn't need friends, not when he held the reins of power in his hands.

And still there was no trace of Robin Fletcher or his son. As each hour passed, the degree of his temper increased until Melanie finally told him while everyone understood his emotional state, he should either hand over his cases for a while or get his shit together in a hurry.

After that, he used all his performance skills to convince people the grieving frantic man was the real C.D. Ellis, but beneath the surface his emotions continued to seethe violently.

****

Robin woke disoriented, unsure at first where she was. Then, scanning the large bedroom she was in and seeing Bobby lying on the pillows, his face still pinched with fear, it all came back to her. Milla. The flight from the house. The call to Zander who without question picked them up in his plane and flew them to safety.

At least for now. They needed to talk, so she knew exactly how much he was willing to help. And she needed to change the color and style of her hair. Would Zander feel comfortable enough to get her what she needed? Maybe he could send one of Guardian's female agents to get what she needed.

Next to her, Bobby shifted. "I have to go to the bathroom."

"Of course you do. Let's get up and get dressed and go find Zander."

Panic slashed across the little boy's face. "He won't make us leave, will he? Where would we go?"

"We're staying right here," she assured him. She hoped. "Let's get moving, and we can ask him questions."

"Is Mommy coming here?" he asked, hope stamped on his face.

"Not today." *Or ever.* "Bobby, your Mommy had an accident before we left, and she didn't wake up."

She dreaded having to give him that news, but she'd put it off as long as she could.

"My Mommy's dead." He whispered the words, pain stamped on his face. "My Daddy hit her, and she never woke up."

How on earth had he seen that?

"I heard them on the balcony and peeked out. Aunt Robin, you won't make me go with him, will you? I hate him. He was always mean to Mommy and me."

She thought her heart was about to break.

"No, honey, you're staying right with me. Forever. Let's have a good breakfast and get moving. Zander is probably waiting for us to make sure we're okay. That we had a good night's sleep. You can trust him, Bobby. I promise you.""

And I hope he meant what he said about helping us.

She pulled clothes from her suitcase, and when the two of them were washed and dressed, they went in search of Zander. They found him in the kitchen, standing at the counter, a mug of coffee on the counter near him and breakfast fixings laid out next to the stove. A small television on the counter was turned to a news channel, and she kept her eyes on it for a news bulletin about Milla's death and/or her disappearance.

"Sorry." Zander spoke in a low tone. "I was just trying to see how big a case this would be and hoped to turn it off before Bobby could see it." He smiled at the little boy. "How about some juice to start the day?"

Bobby looked at Robin. "Is it okay?"

"Of course. We're Mr. Craig's guests. You can have anything you want for breakfast."

"How about bacon and eggs?" Zander suggested.

"Yes, please."

Robin hated that he was so subdued and frightened.

"Coming right up." Zander poured the boy a glass of juice. "Why don't you take it into the living room? You can see all over San Antonio from the big window."

As soon as he was out of the room, Robin moved close to Zander. "After breakfast, we have to find a way to occupy Bobby so you and I can talk."

"Already thought of that. Nick Vanetta, one of the partners, is picking him up and taking him to their ranch. He and Lindsey have a couple of kids, so there'll be plenty there to occupy him."

"Is it safe there for him?" She hated letting him out

of her sight.

"It is. Otherwise I'd never have suggested it." He broke eggs into a bowl. "This story is big enough to have hit all the news channels in less than twenty-four hours," he told her. "C.D. is giving an award-winning performance as the grieving widower and begging for the return of his son.

"Asshole," she muttered.

"We need to keep Bobby away from the television, which is one reason I thought of the ranch."

"I just—" Something on the television screen caught her eye, and her stomach tightened. "Zander, can you turn up the television? Just saw something that isn't good. Hurry, before Bobby comes in here."

The camera had switched back to the reporter. Apparently, the story had gone national on the morning news. A story this big, centering around a powerful criminal defense attorney, wasn't something the police could keep a lid on. While C.D., with his questionable stable of clients, might not be looked on as a pillar of the community, and maybe especially because of that, the story was playing out in full drama on all the morning news programs.

"A nationwide manhunt is on for Robin Fletcher," the reporter told them, "sister of the murdered woman. She is considered a 'person of interest' in the killing of Milla Ellis and the abduction of her nephew."

Robin thought she might throw up. She felt every bit of blood drain from her face.

"Here. Sit." Zander guided her to a chair at the table. "Let me get you some coffee." He set a steaming mug in front of her.

She actually shook when they replayed the tape of

C.D. pleading for his son's release and return. Speaking directly to *her*. Telling *her* he'd help her any way he could.

Yeah, right. He'd help her right into a coffin or, more likely, a roadside grave.

"Robin, no one who knows you will believe it." Zander's voice was low and reassuring. "C.D. is putting on a show to deflect attention from himself. Here. Take a sip."

Her stomach twisted in knots as she listened to the voice with its dramatic presentation. So he'd managed to do it, the clever asshole. Every cop in the country would be looking for them. Not to mention C.D.'s network of thugs.

"I don't know if I thanked you properly for dropping everything and coming to get me." He'd been her only hope.

He crouched next to her and studied her face.

"We had something special," he reminded her. "and—"

"And I threw it away because I was stupid."

"Let's just say I took a vacation from it. Maybe this isn't the time to say so, but Robin? My feelings for you never changed. I always hoped something would happen so we could reconnect."

She looked down at her hands. "I was so afraid you wouldn't take my call."

"Not a chance. No matter what, I'll always be there for you."

But could they recapture what she'd thrown away?

His cell rang, and he pulled it from his pocket to answer. "Nick and Lindsey are here. Let's get Bobby taken care of. Then we'll talk."

****

The security firm C.D. used had people stationed both at his home and office, although he was staying away from the office right now. The grieving husband and all. The vultures were gathering. He'd had to assign a permanent bodyguard to Melanie Jacobs after a zealous reporter nearly knocked her down as she was entering the office that morning.

C.D. felt as if they were all under siege. The only people who didn't seem to be bothered by it were his clients, who often lived their entire lives that way. For once, he could sympathize with them.

Robin Fletcher and Bobby seemed to have been swallowed up by the earth. His own sources yielded nothing. He'd managed to learn she'd left her car behind and rented one, but the rental also seemed to have disappeared off the face of the earth. Frank had called Sawyer McMullen, Robin's boss, innocently looking for the woman, only to be told she hadn't been at work for several days. Prying the name of Robin's friend, Meg Reid, out of him, he'd passed it along to the police, but the woman gave them nothing. In fact, she had slammed the door in the cop's face.

Then Frank reported back that McMullen and Reid were as baffled as everyone else. C.D.'s computer guru found no trace of any place she'd used identification for anything. Except for her bank withdrawal, she'd truly dropped into a black pit. With his own sources yielding nothing, C.D. hoped the damn police had better results. Once they found her, he'd figure out a way to take care of her that eliminated her.

He ground his teeth as he made his daily call to Mac Fontaine, wondering just what the hell they were doing with no visible progress on the case.

"No, Mr. Ellis, we still don't have any leads." Fontaine's voice was not apologetic. He was delivering a statement. Period.

And maybe hoping to catch me off guard.

"I'm beginning to lose patience here, Detective."

"Understandable. Rest assured we're doing our best. We have everyone possible on this." Abruptly, he hung up.

"That cop doesn't like me," he told Frank, who sat across from him. "He was all business, but his tone let me know exactly what he thinks of me."

"So what do you care?" Frank asked. "He's just a dumb cop."

C.D. shook his head. "He's not so dumb, and don't let your mind slip that way. As far as cops like him are concerned, men who get criminals off and make a lot of money doing it are only one step above the criminals themselves. He thinks I'm scum under his feet. He's doing his job, but that's it. And he's not passing along anything from the FBI."

C.D. knew what he was talking about. He sensed the cop was suspicious that his hands might not be absolutely clean in this matter,

Frank raised one eyebrow. "What can he know, anyway? There's no one except that stupid nanny and the housekeeper who might even suspect that you and Mrs. Ellis had...difficulties. And you paid the nanny off enough so she could retire to Europe if she wanted to."

C.D. fiddled restlessly with a pencil. "I promise you that man would be more than happy to pin Milla's death on me if only he had the least smidgen of evidence."

"We took care of that, boss. Every bit of it. There's

nothing left for him to find. Now, all you have to do is sit tight until that bitch sister is found."

"Yeah, right."

"Maybe the U.S. Marshals will track her down," Frank pointed out. "Those guys never give up. Wouldn't that help?"

"No, you idiot." C.D. slammed his hand down on his desk. "You think I actually want her caught? I want to find my son and get rid of Robin Fletcher once and for all. Do you think I want her to talk to anyone? Tell them her story?"

In fact, C.D. was more concerned that he hadn't yet found her himself. That was his top priority. To find her and kill her before she could talk to the police. Once she opened her mouth, nothing he said or did could stop the police from opening everything up again. And that was a chance he couldn't afford to take.

"You don't think they'll be suspicious if you give them a dead body?"

"Not if I do it right."

"Well, we've got a big fat zero with the boss and the girlfriend." Frank pushed himself out of the chair. "I know the cops have talked to Fletcher's neighbors, but maybe someone might remember something. After the fact, you know?"

"Just don't get carried away," Ellis warned. "That's all we'd need is for you to get arrested for roughing up one of her neighbors."

Frank held up his hand. "No rough stuff. Scout's honor. But maybe the cops didn't ask the right questions."

"All right." C.D. threw down the pencil. "Come by later tonight and tell me what you've found. If anything."

The minute Frank left, C.D. picked up the phone and dialed a number he hadn't used in a long time. Frank was good, and the men he used were diligent. But this called for something a little more than that. He didn't care if the police ever found Robin Fletcher as long as *he* did and her body disappeared.

****

Captain Davis leaned back in his chair and looked at his detective sergeant who was straddling a metal chair. Mac Fontaine had been on his squad for five years, recently made sergeant and Davis trusted his judgment and his instincts completely. Although nominally he reported to Lieutenant Jensen, in many instances, he worked directly for the captain of the homicide division.

Davis narrowed his eyes at him, studying the younger man. "What's your take on it, Mac?"

"The C.D. Ellis mess?"

Davis snorted. "Is there another one on the fire right now?" He shook his head. "I don't like that man, and I want to be sure it isn't just normal prejudice for slime balls like him."

"Well, he's not on my Christmas card list, either, but I know what you mean. Something smells, and it isn't the garbage."

"Okay," Davis said. "Let's have it."

"He's too pat," Fontaine said. "His act is too polished. He looks like one of his own witnesses. Says and does all the right things. Shows just the right amount of emotion. I might give him an Oscar, but I wouldn't give him a pass on this."

Davis sighed. "I get the same feeling, but we have absolutely nothing to base this on except instinct."

"The medical examiner said Mrs. Ellis had a lot of

healed injuries and bruises that were still fading," Fontaine pointed out.

"Yeah, but Ellis says his wife was an alcoholic who fell down a lot. Says that's why he had a nanny. Couldn't trust his wife to take care of the child."

Fontaine shrugged. "Plausible. Maybe too plausible. And it seems very strange she had no friends who could corroborate this. Apparently, she never left the house."

"Or he never *allowed* her to leave."

A sharp rap on the door interrupted their conversation.

"Come in," Davis called.

Joel Stetler, Special Agent in Charge—SAC—of the FBI's Seattle office pulled up the room's only other chair. Dressed in khakis and a University of Washington sweatshirt, he looked like anything but the general image of an FBI agent. Davis had worked with him before and both liked and respected the man.

"Are we discussing the topic of the day?" he asked.

Davis nodded and brought him up to speed on the conversation.

Stetler listened carefully. "We've taken Robin Fletcher's life apart from the time she was born, right through the death of her parents in an airplane crash, her sister's ill-fated marriage, and her present situation in Seattle." He shook his head. "The least likely candidate I've ever seen for this kind of thing."

"That's what we were saying," Fontaine agreed. "Here's a woman with everything in the world going for her. Great job. Plenty of friends. Great place to live. No one ever remembers hearing her express anger or jealousy at her sister's situation."

"Except to call C.D. Ellis a brutal asshole," Davis

broke in.

"Right," Stetler agreed. "She wasn't shy about telling people she hated that marriage, but it wasn't because she was jealous. She didn't trust Ellis from here to the door."

"He tried very hard at first to tell us his wife had fallen, but an examination of the body showed someone had inflicted the wounds that killed her. Then Ellis has tossed the blame to Robin Fletcher, claiming there was bad blood between the sisters. The problem was, no one but him and his sidekick, Frank, seemed to know anything about it."

Fontaine crossed his forearms on the back of the chair and leaned his chin on them. "I know it in my bones. He's lying to us about everything, but we've got no way to prove it. No one knows better how to stage a crime scene than that asshole."

"Funny that he's the only one who mentioned her jealousy of her sister," Davis put in. "Everyone else tells a different story. And what about her condo being ransacked? Surely, she didn't do that herself."

"It would help if we could get our hands on her," Stetler pointed out. "Then maybe we could make sense out of all this."

Davis shook his head. "That woman has gone to ground somewhere with that little boy, and we'll be lucky if she surfaces fifty years from now. She's done a professional disappearing act."

"That she has," Stetler agreed.

Fontaine looked from one man to the other. "What am I missing here?"

"She's had help," the FBI man said. "You put a BOLO out for her right away, and we added ours since we first got the call from you guys. Now, if in the whole United States we can't even find her car…"

"She could have sold it. Gotten rid of it," Mac pointed out. He and Davis had gone over and over the vehicle thing.

Stetler shook his head. "Her name would have to appear somewhere, like on the pink slip she transferred."

"Or maybe she just ditched it and bought a new one," Mac suggested. "She cleaned out her bank account. She could pay cash."

"Again, she'd need identification. Which means someone's helped her put together a whole new identity."

Davis leaned forward, resting his elbows on his desk. "You know, that money thing could be looked at in two ways. She could have been planning to snatch the kid and needed the money to start a new life. However she managed it."

"Or," Mac interjected, "she wanted to get her sister and nephew out of there. Even her boss told us that. The money could have been for the three of them."

The men sat and stared at each other, each digesting the material they'd already hashed over a hundred times.

"I can't get anyone in that house to admit to a thing," Davis said at last, disgusted. "They're either too well paid or too frightened. I even threatened the nanny with jail for obstruction of justice and that didn't faze her at all."

"Well." Mac stood up and pushed his chair back in place. "What chaps my britches is that schmuck Ellis might very well have committed the perfect murder and is getting away with it." He grunted. "The way he wears the mantle of the grieving husband and father, even breaking up in court…" He shook his head. "That man will stop at nothing."

"I'd like to nail him just on the charge of being an abominable human being," Davis put in. "You know everything about her life is classic textbook abuse. No friends, alienation from her only relative. Old injuries. And that asshole looks us straight in the face and says the sister killed her."

"He's sure not letting up the pressure about his son," Stetler pointed out. "He calls my office every day."

Davis picked up the cup of cold coffee on his desk, made a face at its bitter taste, and put it down again. "If he's the doting father he pretends to be, I feel for him. But my gut tells me he wants to find that boy so he can get his hands on Robin Fletcher. And make sure she never has a chance to talk to us."

"We'll keep working it," Stetler said. "There's something we need to keep in mind. If we don't find Robin Fletcher before Ellis does, we may never find her at all."

Chapter Six

Robin liked Lindsey and Nick Vanetta on sight. And how much safer could Bobby be than with one of the Guardian Security partners? And without asking questions, Lindsey handed her what she needed to alter her appearance, from hair color to makeup.

Lindsey settled Bobby, who was excited about seeing a real ranch, in a suburban with tinted windows and urged Zander to bring Robin out later. Then they were alone, the silence between them like a yawning abyss.

Robin couldn't believe how she'd jumped into Zander's arms when he'd shown up or the thrum of attraction that was still so strong between them. She knew Zander was trying to keep a lid on it, and she hoped she'd didn't screw this up by doing something stupid. No, wait, she'd already done that by breaking up with him. Could he get past that?

Dummy.

What if Ellis tracked her down and killed her, too? She had to hope—no, pray—that they'd be able to pin it on him without her. Then, when he and his thugs were locked up, she'd feel safer coming forward. But not until then.

Zander refilled their coffee mugs and carried them into the living room, putting them on the coffee table. Robin was wound tighter than a drum, but she knew he had to get the whole story in front of him. And then address the elephant in the room. But apparently, Zander wanted that out in the open first.

"I hadn't planned to jump right into this," Zander told her, studying her face. "And maybe this isn't the right time, considering the circumstances. If it's too much, let me know."

"If what's too much?" She frowned, puzzled.

He blew out a breath. "Me telling you my feelings for you have never changed. I wasn't going to say anything right now, but the fact that you called me tells me there's still something between us. At least, I like to think there is. When I left Seattle, I always planned to wait until the right time and then go back and plead my case to you. Then life just accelerated everything and it's important to me that you know how important you are to me. It hit me when you called me. And we can put it on hold until all of this is wrapped up. First things first."

Emotions swirled in her like a rough wind. Yes, she'd automatically reached out for Zander, knowing she could trust him. And the carefully curried feelings that pushed her to make the call were a big factor. She had to keep them that way for Bobby's sake, but the longer she spent with Zander, the more intense she realized her feelings were. Somehow, she had to make up for her stupidity. Looking at the man, his toned body outlined by a T-shirt and jeans, an early morning scruff highlighting his strong chin, his deep blue eyes snapping with life, she wondered how she could have been such a fool as to let him walk away from her.

She took a mental deep breath.

"Yes, first things first." Because right now, whatever she felt for Zander, Bobby came first.

She rose from the couch and stared out the big picture window with its broad view of the landscape. *San Antonio, Texas in the spring is lovely.* The bluebonnets were blooming everywhere, like a thick carpet of blue. The weather was warm during the day, and last night it had only been slightly cool. A pleasant change from the constant cool. For a moment, she felt a tiny touch of peace, but then she turned back to Zander.

"The abuse was going on for a long time," she began, letting out a breath. "At first, everything seemed fine. But then I noticed Milla always seemed jumpy and she took to wearing long-sleeved tops. I asked her if she had a problem, and she blew it off by telling me Seattle's weather was finally getting to her."

Zander nodded. "A plausible but lame excuse."

"And I was too stupid to see through it. I hadn't wanted her to marry C.D. in the first place, but she was starry-eyed over his money and position and whatever I said fell on deaf ears."

"So when did you realize the truth?"

She took a slow sip of coffee. "I came to pick her up one day, and she was in her room getting dressed. That's the first time I saw the bruises. I was shocked."

"What did she say?"

"Lied through her teeth. Said she'd gotten clumsy and kept bumping into things. It took a long time for me to get at the truth and to discover he blackmailed her into silence by threatening to divorce her and take Bobby away from her."

Zander listened carefully as this time she laid out everything she knew. A muscle ticked in his jaw and fury flashed in his eyes.

"He nearly killed her the last time," she went on,

"which is why I was determined this time to get both her and Bobby out of there. It was the perfect opportunity. C.D. was out of town, but I couldn't get her to leave. Then C.D. came home early, and all hell broke loose. I was damn lucky to get Bobby out of there."

She set her mug down with a shaky hand and drew a breath. Retelling the horror shook her. Unexpectedly, Zander put down his coffee, drew her up from the couch, and folded her into his arms. Shockingly, despite the state of her nerves, heat surged through her, and without thinking, she pressed closer to him.

Cool it, Robin. This is a life-or-death matter.

It shocked her the way she reacted to him, and she wondered what he was thinking.

"Okay." He took a step back. "I talked with my partners this morning, and we've all agreed on two things. Bobby's safety is of prime importance. We'll be doing everything we can to keep him safe and hidden away. and C.D. has to be nailed. We've got our crack computer genius digging up everything he can find on the man. We'll be turning him inside out like dirty clothes."

Robin had to giggle at that.

"Robin, I waited a long time to see you again. I never should have just let you walk away from me but…"

"But you had a life, too. If not for Milla, I would have worked harder to keep you in my life, but I couldn't leave her. I'm just so grateful you said you'd help."

"Gratitude isn't necessary. I'm just glad as hell you reached out to me, although I was getting close to taking a trip to Seattle to plead my case." He took her hand and gave it a gentle squeeze. We'll find what we need to nail him. In the meantime, Bobby will never be alone. Either you or I will be with him or a Guardian agent. He'll be out of the public eye and virtually undetectable."

She blew a breath of relief.

"Thank you. Thank you so much."

"Now, before I call a meeting with the team, I want you to go through all this again. No detail is too small. Can you do that for me?"

"To help Bobby? Anything."

But what would happen when she told him she had witnessed the murder? He'd probably be angry, but she was trying to do her best to distance herself. Her prime motive was protecting Bobby, and she'd lie if she had to, although lying to Zander didn't seem like a very smart thing to do.

Her heart ached for the child. How much anguish did he need in his short little life. She vowed that, in the future, she would do everything she could to bring him joy and secretly keep the memory of his mother alive for him.

Chapter Seven

Zander watched Robin and thought about her nephew. A really cute kid. Bright. Friendly but with an unusual reserve for a child his age. No wonder, with the night he'd been through. And Robin herself, beautiful and tempting, was a bundle of nerves she did her best to disguise. He'd known at once she was hiding a terrible secret but hadn't been fully prepared for her story.

Telling it twice had been draining for her, but finally, he had the entire picture. Or was pretty sure he did. He had to trust that Robin had told him everything, although fear sometimes skewed memories. He had to tamp down the urge to fly to Seattle and throttle C.D. with his bare hands. He never should have let her walk away from him the way he did. It was obvious the situation with her sister was already ongoing. What if he'd pushed a little harder? The position with Guardian Security expanded his opportunities, and he damn sure could have figured a way out of this for her.

But your poor dick was insulted because she chose to stay in Seattle,

"Nick will be hanging out at the ranch today," he told her, "making sure Bobby isn't having a meltdown. But I told Reno I'd call and get him and Zak Delaney out here for a meeting. We need a battle plan, and for that, I have to dig every squiggle of information out of your brain. C.D. Ellis will pull out everything he's got to find

Bobby and keep Milla's death covered up. We need to be one step ahead of him."

"You're sure it's safe to share all this information?" She twisted her hands together.

"They're already dialed into this. I gave Nick the short version when I called him this morning and already set one of our researchers on C.D.'s trail looking for ways to find evidence against him. Now, I need to bring in my other partners so we can do a full court press. Robin, Guardian Security is the best there is, and I would trust every one of them, including the admins, with my life. I promise you. If anyone can fix this, Guardian can."

She blew out a breath and nodded. "Okay. Go ahead and call them."

Zander picked up his cell and punched a number into it. "We're in. Bring your brain and a dozen donuts."

He hung up on Reno Sullivan's laugh. How lucky that he'd landed with what had to be the best security agency on the planet. They'd find a way to nail C.D. Ellis and give Bobby and Robin their lives back.

Robin.

Jesus! He was still as hot for her as the first time he'd met her. Keeping his dick in his pants was going to be an exercise in self-discipline. If only he could steal just one kiss…

Cool it. Business first.

But it was going to be damn hard, just like his poor dick.

Chapter Eight

Robin had expected Bobby to cling to her and not want to be spending his time elsewhere. She had been pleasantly surprised when he'd taken so quickly to the Vanettas, but there was something about them that seemed to reach out to Bobby. Plus, they had two kids of their own and horses that Bobby could ride. It was enough to distract him for the moment. And it gave Robin time to take a breath.

The other Guardian partners—Zak Delaney and Reno Sullivan—arrived shortly after the Vanettas left with Bobby. They were both tall with dark hair, although Reno's was blacker than Zak's and his face was leaner. Coal black eyes highlighted lashes that Robin thought were too sinful for a man, and his face had a chiseled look. His tall body was muscular, and he moved with the grace of a panther.

Zak was leaner, his hair not quite as dark, and his features more chiseled. His hair was a little longer, and he wore a Henley as opposed to a button-down shirt.

There was something about them that gave Robin a secure, settled feeling, just like she had with Nick. These men were tough on the inside and exuded a feeling of strength and force. There was a competence about them that said whatever she needed they could provide it. Five minutes with them and she knew that whatever her problem, they could fix it.

Zander had told her they each had interesting background stories, and she was dying to know what they were.

After.

"We know the first thing is to keep Bobby safe," Reno began. "I want you to know the full forces of Guardian Security are in place to do that. Zak and I discussed it on the way over."

Robin let out the breath she'd been holding. "Yes. That's the priority. But how will you do it? And how much will this cost? I have some money, but this will have to be expensive."

Reno's mouth curved in a smile. "We have the friends and family discount, which is zero."

"Each of the partners has been in a similar situation, one where danger was constant," Zak added. "No matter how much Guardian grows, we consider the partnership a family, so don't worry about the money."

"Zander offered to cover it," Reno went on, "but again. Friends and family. We want to focus on two things—Bobby's safety and pinning Milla's death on C.D. Ellis so that's where our energy goes."

Robin blinked back the tears that welled at the generosity of these men who didn't even know her. They were doing all this on the word of a man she'd mistakenly walked away from. One she realized she desperately needed in her life for a lot of reasons, not the least of which was his protection. "So where do we start?"

"Nick and I discussed this," Reno told her, "and decided for the moment the safest place for Bobby is the Vanetta ranch. Their foreman is always armed, and we can make sure Lindsey is, too."

"Although," Zak added, "we don't believe either will be necessary except maybe for your peace of mind. The ranch is thirty miles outside of San Antonio, and there is no way Ellis will ever be able to make a connection."

"He knows nothing about Zander, right?" Reno asked.

"As far as I know. I never mentioned him to C.D., only Milla, and she would never discuss it with him. And I certainly never brought Zander around for her to see him. I kept my entire personal life away from that environment."

"Good." Reno nodded.

"The next thing is for you to tell us every single thing you can remember about your sister, her marriage to C.D. and all that you've observed. Was he around a lot when you were there visiting your sister?"

Robin shook her head. "Only in the very beginning. Milla was usually alone when I visited her. I think for the wedding and when Bobby was born were the major episodes, plus the very few times I was arriving to visit Milla and he was there but leaving. We never had a conversation."

"Better yet," Zak told her. The less contact he had with you, the fewer clues he would have picked up about where to look for you."

Zander had quietly slipped his hand into hers and gave it a reassuring squeeze.

"But she's high on his list right now," Zander added, "because his choices for Bobby are limited. When he narrows them down, her name will be at the top of the list."

"Did you cover all your tracks when you contacted

Zander?" Reno asked.

"I took the SIM card out of my phone and tossed it after we made contact. I threw the phone itself someplace else." She frowned. "There's no way they can trace my hooking up with Zander at the airport, right?"

"No." Zander shook his head. "Nothing connects that hookup. I made sure the rental was returned by an unremarkable person who left no impression. And if C.D. doesn't know about me, he won't know to look in San Antonio. That's not saying, as he gets more and more desperate, he'll just dig deeper into Robin's life and eventually come up with the connection."

"And we'll be prepared," Reno assured him. "Meanwhile, let's have everything you remember. I have one of our researchers at the office digging into every single thing he can find on C.D., but we need any personal information you can give us."

"Okay." She blew out a breath, grateful for Zander's hand holding hers. "I'll do my best."

Filling them in took more than an hour, to her surprise. She hadn't realized how much she really knew about C.D., but Milla had let a lot of things drop here and there, including things about his office and the people who worked there. And, of course, Frank, the ever-present bodyguard. She was exhausted by the time they finished, but for the first time since the disaster at Milla's, she felt she could draw a deep breath.

And Zander had held her hand the entire time, the warmth and assurance of it seeping into her system.

And something else.

Something totally inappropriate under the circumstances, but something she couldn't ignore. From the moment he touched her, her nipples had hardened into painful peaks and an insistent throbbing hummed between her thighs. She hadn't felt it in a very long time, not since...

Not since the last time she'd been with Zander.

Did he feel it, too? And how could she want him like this when the crisis with Bobby and C.D. Ellis loomed just in front of her? What would she do if he wanted more, just as she seemed to?

"I'll touch base this afternoon and let you know what else we've come up with," Zak told Robin and Zander. "Meanwhile, Robin, you might want to figure out what you want to do about your stuff in Seattle. I'm taking a wild ass guess here that when this is over, you might not want to go back there?"

"Probably not," she agreed. *That depends on Zander.*

"But for right now," Reno told her, "I'd leave everything as it is, so its look as if you're planning to come back. And Ellis probably has eyes on it twenty-four/seven just in case you show up."

"Good point," Zander agreed.

As soon as the men had left, Zander reset the automatic locks and turned to Robin. It seemed so natural for him to rest his arms on her shoulders and draw her closer to him. She held her breath, waiting to see what he had to say, the heat generated between them a palpable thing. They stood that way for what seemed like a long time before their mouths made contact.

She couldn't have said who moved first but it didn't seem to matter. The kiss was unexpectedly incendiary, a contact that went on and on and on. Her breathing became unsteady, and when he pulled her against his body, the press of her breasts set all her responses on fire.

Then tongues became involved, sweeping against each other like a curtain of heat.

Zander pulled Robin's body against his so she could feel every outline of him, including the hard cock pushing against the fly of his jeans. He ran his hand up and down her back, his tongue exploring even more until they both had to breathe.

"Well." She took a step back and blew a little breath. "That was…"

"Even better than it used to be," he finished. "Better than…well, let's say better than the best. But Robin, if you want me to forget it, just say so."

"That would be impossible."

"I've been trying to keep a lid on my feelings since the night you told me Texas was too far away from everything for you."

"And that's changed," she told him. "I want you to know that."

"I'm in this all the way with you," he assured her. "Wherever it takes us." He squeezed both of her hands.

For the first time since she'd fled Seattle, Robin felt a tiny lessening of the tension and fear. If anyone could make this okay, it was Zander, for both her and Bobby.

****

"Still nothing." C.D. slammed his fist on his desk.

In the past few days, his self-control had begun to fray around the edges and his anger had made itself evident more and more frequently. He'd stayed away from his clients, but he couldn't do that much longer. They were getting antsy along with his associates. It wouldn't do to let anyone see the outer layer of ice had cracked.

Frank had finally gotten him out of the house and

into his office. The man was around most of the time, and he felt like a tiger with his tail in a trap. At least once a day, Melanie called and threatened to either quit or shoot him. He thanked the lord she hadn't, because she was the backbone of the office, the one who kept him sane and on track.

Sitting in the chair across from him now, Frank watched him, his eyes assessing the level of today's anger. Since *that night*, he'd hardly been away from C.D.'s side, except to handle specific errands.

"It's only been a couple of days," Frank reminded him. "You've got an army out searching. It'll happen."

"He's slowly coming unglued," Melanie had commented more than once. "Somehow, we have to keep him together."

"You need to cut down on the temper tantrums, C.D.," Frank told him now, "and put on the mantle of grief. *That's* what you should be parading around. Think how well it'll play with the juries."

A muscle twitched in Ellis's cheek as he fought to calm himself. "All well and good, but you're forgetting one thing. As long as Robin Fletcher is alive, she can point the finger at me for Milla's death."

"And you think people will believe her?" Frank asked. "After the number you did throwing all the blame on her?"

"Frank." Ellis's voice was filled with aggravated patience. "I know how the cops work. They won't just take my word about what I suppose happened. Even if they find her and arrest her, they'll still drag everything up again. She'll run her mouth, and some smart cop will decide to see if she's right."

"There's no evidence," Frank reminded him.

"I've seen people executed on less." He stared at Frank. "But it's not the cops I want finding her. Don't we have anyone out there with half a brain who can find one stupid female and a little boy? And get the job done?"

"You know we have contacts everywhere in the country looking."

"I'm tired of looking." C.D. pushed back from his desk. "It's time for finding. The only way that bitch could disappear like that is if she had professional help. If that is the case, I'd know about it. I know everyone in this country who can create new identities. God knows we've used them often enough."

Frank shook his head. "Not all of them, C.D. You know there's got to be a few we don't have on our radar."

"Then find them," he ordered. "Jesus. A woman and a little boy can't hide forever. The kid has to go to school. She has to make a living. Tell everyone to get off their asses and dig harder."

He raked his fingers through his expensively cut hair. This was turning into the worst nightmare of his life. He had one goal—to kill Robin Fletcher. If his son ended up being collateral damage, he'd have to deal with that. Right now, he just wanted that woman dead, however it was accomplished.

His intercom buzzed, and he pressed the speaker button. "What?"

"Your new client is here. Along with his...entourage."

He could tell from Melanie's voice just what kind of entourage it was. The client was a Texas millionaire who lived a lifestyle out on the edge. He'd made his money in the dot.com market before it tanked, then turned it into even more money. Some said he was heavily involved in money laundering. Rumors of drugs, sex parties, and other wild activities surrounded him, but no one had ever been able to prove anything.

Except perhaps the man's third wife, who apparently had filed for divorce, then took a header off their third-floor balcony at their elaborate gated estate north of San Antonio. The police were discounting the story he'd given them and were looking at him hard for the murder. Unwilling to leave himself unprotected, he'd called C.D. in the middle of the night, wired him a retainer, and flown to Seattle on his private jet.

"If I'm going to be defended on a murder charge," he said in their late-night phone call, "I want the best. Charge whatever you want. Money's no object."

All right, then. C.D. certainly knew all about men who murdered their wives, so who better to do this job than him? It was time to pull himself together and go to work.

"Go make calls," he told Frank. "Tell everyone I'm now offering a million-dollar bonus to the first person who takes care of this for me."

Frank's eyes popped. "Jesus. You'll have every trigger finger in the country on the prowl for this."

An icy smile twisted C.D.'s lips. "That's exactly what I want."

"You want me to tell the media, too?"

C.D. pursed his lips, then shook his head. "Not yet. Let's see what happens without that. Now get moving."

Chapter Nine

It was obvious to the two of them that they had a hard time keeping their hands off each other all day. Robin gave thanks that she was so focused on Bobby and the danger to him that she was able to control herself. They spent the day going over again everything she'd told Reno and Zak plus all the details she could dig up in her mind on C.D. Ellis.

"The man is a devil," she kept repeating. "I tried so hard to talk Milla out of marrying him, but he swept her off her feet. Rich, handsome, and attentive. What more could she ask? Right? She and I are so different. She never focused on the future except to find a husband. And look what she got." Robin swallowed some coffee. "By the time she listened to me, it was too late, and she was terrified to leave him. She was sure he'd find a way to take Bobby away from her."

"We're not going to let him get his hands on the boy," Zander promised her. "You have my word."

The sexual tension was almost palpable as they worked through the day. Robin repeated whatever details she remembered about every visit with her sister that she was sure by this time they were engraved in her brain. But over and above everything was the heat simmering between her and Zander. How would they keep it under control until this situation was resolved? And did they really have to?

She was glad when Lindsey Vanetta delivered Bobby at the end of the day to ease the simmering heat and tension. He was bouncing with excitement, his face flushed, his body practically shaking.

"I rode a horse today, Aunt Robin," he told her for the fifth time. "And I played with two little kids, and they liked me. And we had hot dogs for dinner made on the grill. They were so good."

He was hopping around on one foot, waving his arms. His face was flushed, but Robin chalked that up to the excess of excitement.

She supervised his bath and got him settled in bed. His face was still a little flushed, and she thought he felt a little warm, but again, she chalked it up to the excitement of the day.

"Miss Lindsey said I can go back tomorrow," he told her. "Can I? Is it all right? It's so fun out there."

"As long as you behave yourself," she told him. "Okay."

He nodded. "I'll be really, really good."

But she conveyed her worries to Zander.

"I just hope he doesn't have some kind of bug," she told him. "He could have picked up something in the motel or rental car. Or even at school before I took him from the house. Milla was a good mother, or as good as she could be. Always doing what she could to protect him. But she might not have noticed something, as nervous as she was about C.D."

Zander was throwing a later dinner together when his cell rang.

"It's Reno," he said, looking at the readout. "Maybe he's got word on something." He pushed the Answer button. "Yeah, buddy, what's up? What the fuck?"

Robin saw his face tighten with tension.

He listened for another moment. "Okay. We'll do whatever we have to. Get your feelers out for whatever you can find. We need to meet again tomorrow."

"What is it?" she asked as soon as he disconnected.

"I don't know any other way to tell you except to spit it out. Ellis's put out a million-dollar reward for information leading to finding Bobby."

Robin almost stopped breathing. "He'll have the whole country looking for Bobby."

"Including the scumbags who thrive on this. But that's not all."

Robin wasn't sure she wanted to hear the rest. "What could be worse?"

"He's put the same price tag on your head. He apparently did another press conference playing the grieving widower enraged that you killed your sister, the wife he loved so much."

Robin was afraid she was going to throw up. "Zander, everyone with an itchy trigger finger will be looking for me."

"But we aren't going to let anything happen to you. Count on it. Guardian has the best security bar none."

He lifted her from the chair where she'd been watching him, hands beneath her elbows, and pulled her toward him. What started out as a gentle hug turned into full body contact. Robin threw her arms around him and plastered himself against his body. She didn't care about the timing or anything else. She was terrified, both for herself and Bobby, and this man was her safe harbor.

And more. Much more. How had she ever walked away from him?

Before she realized it, they were kissing again,

tongues tangling, bodies pressed so tightly together she could feel the hard, thick length of his cock pressed against her sex. Needing to be more intimate, she wrapped her legs around his hips and pressed so hard against him that she wanted to rip away the layers of clothing separating them. The hell with waiting. She could be dead before this was resolved and never had a chance at this relationship.

Zander walked them over to the stove and turned off the burners.

"Think Bobby's sound asleep," he murmured in her ear, gently nipping her ear lobe.

"I'm sure, but let's just check on him."

She slid from his body and headed for the bedroom Bobby was using. The two-bedroom condo was set up with the guest room at one end of a hall and the master suite at the other. Zander went with her as she checked on the little boy.

"He's sound asleep," she told him, then pressed her hand to his cheek and forehead. "He still seems a little warm to me, but I'm sure it's the day's excitement. We can check on him again later."

He nipped her ear lobe. "Later."

He took her hand and led her to the master suite, turning on only the bedside lamp so the room was bathed in soft light. For a moment, a sudden attack of nerves washed over her. This would not be the first time she and Zander had sex, and it had always been great. But this was different. *They* were different. What if—

Stop it! This will be better than ever.

Zander slid his hands up her arms and brushed a kiss across her lips. "I've been waiting a long time for this. And it will be like brand new."

She traced the seam of his lips with her tongue, relishing the taste of him. Heat seared its way through her body, and she pressed close to him again.

He slid his hands down to her waist, then up along her sides until they were cupping her breasts through her thin blouse. When he pinched her nipples between thumb and forefinger, tingles shot through her and she moaned. She felt the dampness between her legs and pressed her sex hard against the thick outline of his cock.

They stood like that for a long moment, Zander teasing her nipples while she rubbed against his hard shaft. She trembled slightly when he tugged her blouse from her waistband and slid his hard, muscular hands along her skin until he reached her bra. A flick of his fingers and he had it unhooked. Moments later, her top and the bra were tossed to the floor and she was naked from the waist up.

Zander cupped her breasts with his palms and bent his head to draw one taut nipple into his mouth, sucking on it hard. She felt it all the way to the heart of her sex, enough so she had to squeeze her legs together against the ripples suddenly rolling through her inner muscles. When he scraped his teeth along the taut bud, heat shot through her. She gripped his shoulders, hard, to keep her balance, her body trembling as he turned his attention to her other breast.

When he took her nipple in his mouth, lightly grazing the taut bud, heat shot through her and her legs trembled.

"We have too many clothes on," he murmured, nipping her ear lobe.

"You have more on than I do," she pointed out.

"We need to fix that right now."

He took a step away from her and yanked the covers back onto the bed. Then he undid the zipper on her jeans and shoved them and her bikini briefs down her legs. His fingertips trailed through the lips of her sex as he did so, ratcheting up her desire even more.

Then they were both naked and Robin feasted on the sight of his nakedness—flat stomach, hard abs, dark curls sprinkled over his chest, barely covering the dark brown nipples and arrowing down to a thickness that surrounded his obviously aroused cock. She couldn't help herself, reaching between them to close her fingers over the erect shaft. She was rewarded when he sucked in his breath and a little groan rolled from his mouth.

But then he wrapped his fingers around her wrist and drew her hand away. "Keep doing that, and it will all be over before it starts." With a smooth movement, he lifted her and placed her on the edge of the bed, feet touching the floor, spread her legs, and knelt between them. "I've wanted to do this from the minute we reconnected."

Gently opening the lips of her sex, he gave the damp flesh a long, slow lick. His hum of satisfaction vibrated through her. She tried to squeeze her legs together, but his broad shoulders kept them wide apart as he did wicked things with his tongue. He took long, slow licks of the sensitive flesh, then swirled the tip of his tongue around her throbbing clit. Her inner muscles quivered and flexed with need.

Zander used the tip of his tongue to trace the line of her slit before easing it inside her heated flesh. She clamped the walls of her sex around that clever tongue and rocked back and forth, trying to urge him to go faster and harder, but he seemed to have set a pace and wasn't budging.

"More," she cried. "Please."

The rumble of his laughter pulsated against her inner flesh, causing it to clench even more.

"Not hurrying this, sweetheart. I've dreamt about it for too many nights to rush it and miss one delicious taste or one hot reaction."

That said, he thrust his tongue inside her again, then drew it out, dragging it against the muscles and over her clit.

Robin couldn't stand it. She lifted her heels and dug them into the edge of the mattress, pushing herself against Zander's very talented tongue and letting ripples of pleasure ride over her. He responded by thrusting his tongue back inside her, deeper and harder, driving her to the edge of pleasure.

She felt the orgasm building and pushed against Zander's tongue. He responded by pinching her clit, a firm squeeze, and she came with an explosion that rocked her body. He thrust his fingers inside her and took her clit in his teeth. Spasm after spasm gripped her until at last the tension in her body eased and she let her legs fall wide apart again.

When she opened her eyes, Zander was watching her with a hungry look but a questioning one, too.

"Okay?" he asked.

"Better than, but I hope that's only the first act."

His laugh was a low, sexy rumble.

"Oh, sweetheart, you can count on it. I've got a lot of waiting stored up."

"But—but you didn't even know if we'd ever see each other again."

"Now that's where you're wrong. If all this hadn't happened, I was about at the point where I was heading for Seattle and pleading my case again." He slid up her body and pressed his mouth to hers.

She could taste herself on his lips, a sensation that kindled the heat in her body.

"For real?" she asked when he lifted his head.

"Definitely. We had—have—something special, Robin. I didn't plan on just letting you disappear from my life." He cupped her face in his palms. "And we have a lot of time to make up for."

He pressed a long, slow kiss to her lips, easing his tongue inside and moving it around in lazy swirls.

And just like that, she was aroused again.

And so was he, the hard, long, length of his cock pressing against the inside of one thigh.

Wriggling to shift position, Robin slid up on the bed and dragged Zander with her. When he was stretched out full length beside her, she rose to her knees and took his cock in one hand, cupping his balls with the other. She stroked the hard length of flesh, feeling it swell even more as she moved her hand up and down.

Zander dug his fingers into the cheeks of her ass, anchoring himself to her.

"I want to be inside you," he growled.

"Soon," she told him as she continued to stroke and squeeze.

"Now," he growled. "I don't want this to go to waste."

With a swift movement of his body he rolled to the side, dislodging her, and reached into the nightstand drawer.

Robin blinked when he pulled out a string of three condoms, reminding her that she hadn't expected him to be celibate while they were apart. He was a man with a healthy sexual appetite, and she hadn't expected they'd ever see each other again.

Swiftly and expertly, he ditched the wrapper and rolled the condom onto his thick cock. Then he arranged her on her back, bending her knees so they were wide apart and prodding her opening with the head of his dick. She was already so wet and slick that he eased himself right inside, and she gasped at the feeling of fullness.

Oh, god!

Her inner muscles clamped down on him, squeezing his hard length, and she could already feel the tremors building inside her.

He rode her hard but slow, taking his time, drawing every response from her he could. She wound her legs around him and pulled her body tight to his as the spasms built and built inside her.

The orgasm, when it came, was a powerful explosion that rocked them both. They shuddered together with the effect of it, her inner muscles milking him and squeezing him. It went on and on until every spasm had been rung from her. She slid her legs down his muscular body and cupped his face in her palms.

When she looked at Zander, he was smiling, a look of deep satisfaction on his face.

"That was worth waiting for," he said at last. "How about you?"

"More than." And she meant it.

The look he gave her reached deep inside her.

"This is more than just sex, Robin. It's important for you to believe me. I never stopped wanting you. Thinking about you."

"I'm so sorry I—"

He touched two fingers to her lips.

"That's done. In the past. Our future starts now." He gave her a gentle hug. "And includes Bobby."

And that brought it all back to her. "No matter what happens, I will never let C.D. get his hands on him again."

"He won't be able to," Zander assured her, "because we're going to make sure he pays for Milla's murder and rots in jail."

Robin hugged him, hard. "When you say it like that, I believe you. And speaking of Bobby, I need to take a minute to check on him. See if he's still running a temperature."

"I'm sure he's fine, but yes, you should see how he's doing. And Robin?"

"Yes?"

"It's going to work out. Guardian will make sure you and Bobby are safe and C.D. gets his due punishment."

The way he looked at her, how could she not believe him?

Chapter Ten

By morning, if Bobby had been running a temperature, it was gone and he was bouncing with anticipation of another day at the Vanetta ranch. Robin still had misgivings, but with his symptoms gone, she had no reason to keep him home. And Reno had called to say they had a shit pile of stuff his people had dug up on C.D. Ellis that he wanted to go over with her.

"We have some decisions to make," he told her, "and we all need to be fully informed before we move forward."

"I'm ready," she assured him, "as long as we keep Bobby safe."

Zander had tried to feed her breakfast, but she didn't have much of an appetite. Except, of course, for the kiss he gave her when she came into the kitchen after seeing Bobby off. She had slept with him the night before but slipped into her own room, not ready yet to expose Bobby to their relationship. They needed to get proof that C.D. had murdered Milla first and that he was solidly out of Bobby's life before that. But the kiss when they were alone? It settled her world.

She had just finished her toast when Reno arrived. She filled coffee mugs for all of them and carried them to the dining room table. Reno opened the large briefcase he was carrying and removed thick stacks of printouts.

"I brought copies of everything we dug up so we'd

each have them," he explained. "That way what we discuss will be right in front of each of us. Robin, that brother-in-law of yours is a real piece of work"

"Tell me about it," she snorted.

"I have to say, the more I learn about C.D. Ellis the happier I am that you're away from him. If he didn't have the money he's got, you can be sure he'd be rotting away in some jail by now. He breaks all the rules and gets away with it. And his good right hand, Frank, does all his dirty work and cleans up after it."

A shiver raced down Robin's spine as she remembered her few encounters with the man. She knew that Milla had been afraid of him and usually kept Bobby in her room with her when C.D. was out of the house but Frank was hanging out. That man would do anything for C.D., even kill if necessary. Something he may already have done."

"It had to be hard for your sister," Zander commented as he slid into the chair next to her. "Living in an environment like that is frightening."

Robin nodded. "As soon as she realized C.D. was using Bobby as leverage against her, threatening to harm the boy to keep her under his thumb, she did everything she could to make sure he was never alone with C.D. I got the feeling from something she said that this was the cause of much of his abuse where she was concerned. That boy was a possession to him, and he didn't like people keeping his possessions away from him."

"That ties in with some things we've unearthed," he told them. "If you look at the first group of printouts, you'll see that your sister had several doctor visits, but they were all house calls."

"What do you mean? Was she sick or something?"

"Did you have stretches of time when she refused to see you? Stayed locked up in the house?"

"Well, yes," Robin nodded. "But she always told me it was the flu or a migraine or something." She clenched her fists. "I knew C.D. was abusing her, although I had no way to prove it without her cooperation. That's what this is about, right?"

Reno nodded. "We found the doctor that he used for the 'incidents' involving Milla. Not his regular doctor, but one who owed him a favor. That was easy enough. Getting the rest of the information took a little bit of pressure, but he finally coughed it up. He willingly made house calls every time Milla was hurt and kept his mouth shut for the exorbitant fees he was paid."

"He could lose his license, right?" Robin asked. "Maybe even go to jail?"

"We might have promised him that wouldn't happen. That we were just looking for leverage against C.D. Robin. I don't know if you're aware of the extent of the abuse."

Nausea crept up in her throat.

"More than I wanted to be but obviously not enough. Milla just refused to discuss it with me. I know she was afraid if she brought it out in the open that C.D. would find a way to cover it up. Then he'd divorce her and take Bobby. I didn't know what to do short of kidnapping the two of them."

"I think we're all aware of the difficult situation," Reno assured her. "We looked into C.D.'s background, too, examining some of his cases and the clients he represents. Most of them barely make it on the right side of the law, but they've got the money to pay exorbitant legal fees to keep them out of jail. C.D. has a rough reputation, but he also carries a lot of power that he's built over the years. People are afraid to get on the wrong side of him, which is why he's been able to pull off so many crooked deals."

"I know he has a fat client list of heavy hitters," Robin told them.

"True." Reno nodded. "And none of them are squeaky clean. He's built a practice of very wealthy people whose business activities are, shall we say, on the shady side. He always manages to find a way to keep them out of trouble and out of prison, no matter what they've done."

"And they're so grateful they've provided him with a big power base," Zander guessed.

"Got it in one. The judges know he's skirting the law, but he never crosses the line, so there's nothing they can do about it. A lot of them would love to nail his hide to the wall." He handed each of them another folder of papers. "Look through these bios. Those clients have their own contacts out in the world and, Robin? He's using their power in his hunt for you and Bobby."

Fear surged through her. "What if he finds me?"

"Not gonna happen." Reno shook his head. "I tell you that because I believe you need to have all the facts at hand. Guardian Security knows what it's doing. We just have to set up a plan here, and that's what we're doing."

"Like what? And is it okay for Bobby still to go out to the Vanettas?"

"Right now, that's the best place for him. You have no known connection to them, so it's not a place anyone would look. And it keeps him busy during the day, so he's not asking questions."

"But I know C.D. has at least one client in Texas,"
she told him, "although I don't remember where. Just
that he was a big deal. Milla had met him when they
hosted a dinner for him, and she didn't much like him. If
he's someone who crosses paths with the Vanettas, then
Bobby isn't safe."

"The man you're thinking of lives in Houston,"
Reno told her. "He came up in our search of Ellis's
clients. But Texas is a big state, and we have no intention
of taking Bobby to Houston. The guy might as well live
in the Arctic. Trust me."

It was another hour before they finished reviewing
all the materials Reno had brought. By that time, Robin
was developing a headache and wishing she and Bobby
could just disappear into a black hole.

"Robin, C.D. Ellis is a high-profile person, and the
murder of his wife and disappearance of his son are the
kind of stuff the media are addicted to. As long as they
keep it alive, the police will still be all over it."

"Like what?" she asked.

"Everything a case like this demands," he explained
to her. "Sending out a general notice once a month.
Checking with all their snitches. Rehashing what
happened that night. That kind of stuff."

"And if the police find me? The first person they'll
tell is C.D."

"Not necessarily. You let us handle it. I just wanted
you to have all the information we do." Reno reached out
and squeezed her hand. "In case anything rings bells in
your mind, something that might give us a clue as to
where C.D. will have people looking. And we're going
to draw up a plan for daily activities. The big thing is the
two bounties of a million bucks each that Morgan has put

on your head and Bobby's. Word is he's reached out to every crooked contact he has, and it's certainly generated a lot of interest. It's got people crawling out of every hole searching for you both. I'm sure he's sent a photo to everyone, so we need to keep you out of sight."

"And we'll keep Bobby busy and tucked away so there's no danger of spotting him," Zander added.

Robin rubbed her forehead where the headache was beginning to build. She had every faith in Zander and Guardian Security, but they were right that C.D. had tentacles everywhere. Was Guardian big enough and powerful enough to battle him?

They spent another hour mapping strategies and discussing the best way to follow the hunt for Robin and Bobby. By then, Robin was ready to collapse.

"Come lie down," Zander told her. "You're tighter than a rubber band. Come on. Let me help you relax."

"I feel as if there's something I should be doing," she protested.

"There is. Lying down and letting me get the tension out of those muscles. Come on."

He led her to his bedroom where he coaxed her to lie down, removing her shoes and tucking a pillow beneath her head. The kneading of his fingers began to loosen the knots in her neck and upper body, and after a while, she actually began to relax. But she knew that was only temporary. She'd be a bundle of nerves until the whole situation was resolved and C.D. was someplace where he couldn't hurt them.

She was relieved when Nick delivered Bobby at the end of the day without incident and hugged him until he squirmed to get out of her grasp. She wondered if she'd ever be able to let him go to live a normal life, even when this was all over.

In the morning when she woke him, his face was flushed. Zander found a thermometer in his bathroom so she could take his temperature, and she was disturbed to see it hovered just above one hundred degrees.

"I think you'd better stay home today, kiddo," she told him. "We don't want to take a chance on your getting sick."

"But I feel fine," he protested. "I do."

"And we want to keep it that way. Just humor me. Tomorrow, it will probably be gone."

She hoped.

"Does he get sick often?" Zander asked. "Do you know if he has any chronic conditions?"

"James never mentioned anything besides allergies. I know he gets shots for them periodically, but that's not a big deal, right?"

"Not usually. Let's see what happens after today. I won't let anything happen to him, I promise you."

She appreciated the fact that Zander devoted the entire day to keeping the little boy occupied. He even made a trip to a big box store where he snagged some children's aspirin as well as some games, and the three of them spent that day engrossed in one activity or another.

"Don't you have work to do?" Robin asked him. "Surely, you can't stay home all day playing board games. Doesn't Guardian have things for you to do?"

"This is what they have for me to do," he told her. "Keeping you safe is my only priority." He took one of her hands and gave it a gentle squeeze, sending a shaft of heat through her body.

Bobby seemed much better when she tucked him

into bed that night, but the next morning the fever was back again.

"I'm worried," she told Zander. "Except for the allergies, he's always been a healthy little kid. I don't even remember him getting a cold. I hope this isn't a bug in his system. Or something else."

"Let's give him another day," Zander suggested, "and see where we are then. I'm calling Lindsey to tell her he's staying home with us today. If nothing has changed by tomorrow, we'll get a doctor in."

She tensed at the words.

"Doctor visits leave paper trails," she pointed out. "Will whoever you hook us up with be willing to skip the obvious questions?"

"We have a great doctor who only asks medical questions," he assured her. "Trust me not to put Bobby in any danger."

But a moment seldom went by that she didn't feel the evil of C.D. Ellis riding her shoulder.

By late afternoon, it was obvious Bobby's fever not only wasn't going away but had inched a degree higher, and Robin was a nervous wreck.

"I'm calling the doctor," Zander insisted. "He's a friend of mine who specializes in critical pediatric diseases, but sometimes, we need a doctor off the book and Gage is our go-to guy. Especially when we need to be beyond discreet. There won't be any paper trail here."

The moment Robin met Gage Hollander, she began to breathe easier. He seemed to be cut from the same mold as everyone else—tall, muscular, self-confident, and good-looking. His attitude put her at ease at once, even though introducing a stranger into the situation made her nervous as hell. But he was great with Bobby from the beginning, joking with him as he examined him and making him laugh.

"It's okay, Aunt Robin," Bobby told her. "I'm used to doctors poking me."

"Oh?" And what exactly did that mean. "Has that happened a lot?"

He shrugged. "Just when Mommy wanted to make sure I was okay."

Which didn't really answer the question. She had an uneasy feeling there was something more going on here than a case of the sniffles and a low-grade temperature.

"Well?" she asked when the examination was finished.

"I'd say allergies would be the easiest answer," he told her, "but I'd like to run some tests to make sure."

Every muscle in Robin's body tensed. "You mean take him to a lab or something?"

"There's a very good one I use right near here," he assured her.

Robin looked at Zander. "I don't—"

Gage and Zander exchanged glances.

"I take it this is a special patient like most of mine are?"

Zander nodded. "We need to be so discreet that no one knows we exist."

"No problem." He smiled at Robin. "I'm sure you can tell this isn't our first rodeo. Leave it to me."

"But don't you have to—"

Gage held up a hand.

"I owe Guardian a debt I can never repay. Whatever you need me to do, I can get it done. Meanwhile, our first priority is to make sure this young man doesn't have anything more than the sniffles."

He joked with Bobby while he drew blood from the boy's arm, a procedure that could have been a lot more stressful if he hadn't kept Bobby distracted. And Zander sat beside Bobby, teasing him and telling jokes until the process was complete. Finally, Gage Hollander packed the labelled test tubes into a padded, zippered case.

"I'll put a rush on these," he told Robin and Zander. "The lab I'm using knows what to do."

"And no one will be able to trace this back to Bobby." Robin had to make sure of that. She was all too aware that information wasn't as secure on the Internet as people thought.

"You have my word on this." He smiled at her. "I'd tell you not to worry, but if Guardian has you as a client, that sort of goes with the territory. All their clients worry. But I promise you, all the information is secure."

"When will you have results for us?" Zander wanted to know.

"Two days at the most," Gage told him. "Meanwhile, keep up the aspirin and fluids, and keep him at home."

"I can't go to the ranch?" Distress washed across Bobby's face.

"Just for a couple of days," Robin assured him. "But you and Zander and I can play lots of games to pass the time. We'll have fun. You'll see."

But Bobby didn't look like he thought it was fun and she knew they had a couple of rough days ahead of them. She settled Bobby with a juice box in front of the television, choosing a cable channel with children's programs. She was afraid to turn it to any of the regular channels, worried a news item about Milla would flash on the screen. Then she joined the men near the front door.

"Everything will be fine," Gage told her, giving her a reassuring smile.

"People always say that just before the other shoe drops," she told the man.

"And when it does, we'll take care of it. You'll hear from me in forty-eight hours or less. And when I get the lab results, I'll send whatever medication is indicated over to you. We'll get this young man taken care of."

"I don't know how to thank you," she told the man.

"No thanks necessary.." He shook hands with them both and then he was gone.

Zander closed the door after him and set the electronic locks and the alarm system. Then he drew Robin into his arms. "It will be fine, I promise," he assured her. "Whatever happens, we'll keep Bobby safe."

"I feel as if I've dumped a whole barrel of trouble on you that you don't need."

He kissed her forehead, his lips warm against her skin.

"I need whatever you give me, good or bad," he assured her. "I'll say it again. My biggest mistake was letting you walk away from me. That won't happen again. Count on it. You and Bobby are in my life to stay."

"You weren't counting on a ready-made family," she pointed out to him.

"I want you and whatever comes with you. And I'm not about to let C.D. Ellis get his hands on Bobby again. Once that man is in jail, Guardian's attorneys will set the legal process in motion to sever that relationship altogether."

"Promise me that will happen."
"You have my word."

Chapter Eleven

Lunch was far from a relaxed meal. Bobby, still fighting whatever was wrong with him, had no appetite, despite the plate of his favorite hot dog and fries Robin had made for him. She merely picked at her food.

"I hope we get the test results soon," she told Zander in a low voice, setting her fork down on her plate.

"You heard Gage. He'll rush them through as fast as he can."

She glanced over at Bobby, still playing with his food.

"How about a nap, kiddo?" she asked. "I bet you'll feel better when you wake up."

"When can I go back to the Vanettas?" he asked, a whine edging his voice.

"As soon as Dr. Hollander gives the go ahead. I bet it won't be more than a few days."

"It's boring here," he told her.

"But we're going to find out for sure what's making you sick, and Gage will be able to help us make you better. Now, how about taking a nap, and when you wake up, we'll have milk shakes and play any board game you want?"

"Okay." But he answered with a distinct lack of enthusiasm.

"Come on. Let's get you settled."

When she finished tucking him in, making sure to

give him a couple of aspirin, she went in search of Zander. He had cleared away the remnants of lunch and was watching television in the den.

"Take a look at this," he told her. "There must be an epidemic."

The headline scrawling across the bottom of the screen shouted, "Millionaire Accused of Wife Killing." She sat down next to Zander, glad when he took her hand in his as she read the ugly story of Jason Delaware and the death of his wife.

According to the news, Delaware had been out of town and his wife had been home alone that night with only the housekeeper on premises. The housekeeper told police Lynn Delaware had been drinking all evening until she went upstairs to the master suite. Delaware claimed when he came home, he found his wife's body on the patio, three floors below the master bedroom balcony. The assumption was she'd gone out onto the balcony drunk, lost her balance, and fell.

The police, however, had other ideas. Although they were not releasing any details, the chief of police said in a press conference they had reason to believe it was actually murder. Jason Delaware was high on their suspect list, and the chief claimed they were taking a hard look at him and what really happened, digging into the Delawares' private life.

Apparently rich men are murdering their wives all over the country. Why is that such a shock to me?

Her eyes were drawn to the photograph of the man.

"He looks so much like C.D.," she told Zander. "He's got the same classic, cold, arrogant good looks. The same cruel look about the eyes and mouth. I never saw what appealed to Milla. I guess the way he swept her off her feet and lavished money on her. I always had the feeling Frank, C.D.'s right hand man, urged him to get married to soften his image."

"And I'm sure it helped when he entertained clients," Zander added.

"If only they knew."

She would never, ever forget hiding on the balcony at her sister's house that night. Afraid to make a move. Listening to C.D. batter Milla with his fists. Hearing her sister's cries, her pleading voice. Then the sickening thud, followed by the frightening image of Milla lying like a broken doll on the floor.

Every waking moment, Robin was haunted by the fact she hadn't burst into the room and somehow stopped the brutality, gotten between Milla and C.D. and managed to get her sister out of there. She was sure she'd have nightmares about that for the rest of her life.

It killed her that C.D. hadn't been arrested or even charged. Somehow, he'd managed to fool the police and throw the blame onto her. While she was hiding out in San Antonio, he was living the high life and playing the grieving widower and father.

Asshole.

But apparently Jason Delaware wasn't as smart as C.D. He wasn't going to walk away from this as easily as C.D. had. At least one woman would have retribution for her abuse and death.

Robin spent the rest of the day trying to keep Bobby amused when he woke from his nap and trying not to obsess about the lab results they were waiting for. When they finally had him tucked away for the night, Zander took her hand and led her to the bedroom.

"You're wound up tighter than a drum," he told her,

fingers rubbing her shoulders as they walked. "Come lie down, and let me help you relax."

"But Bobby…"

"Is sound asleep, and with those aspirin in him, he's good for the night. At least a good long nap. Come on. You're making yourself sick. You won't be any good to him if you're out of commission."

Reluctantly, she let him lead her to the bedroom, protesting slightly when he helped her out of her blouse and jeans, tossing her shoes to the side. When he had her stretched out face down on the sheets, he resumed kneading her muscles with his fingers. At first, Robin had to force herself to relax, but after a while, she felt the tight muscles begin to unwind and relax.

Zander worked his way from her shoulders down the length of her spine, pressing and squeezing each area. Halfway down her back, he unhooked her bra and somehow managed to slip it from her body without disturbing her much. Then he moved his hands to her waist and hips, using the same gentle massaging touch.

At some point, as her body relaxed more and more, she felt a tingling in her nipples and tiny spasms set up between her thighs. When he cupped the cheeks of her ass and squeezed them, the heat that had been slowly building in her began to build even more. She tried to squeeze her thighs together, but Zander gently nudged them apart.

"Uh uh. Not yet."

A soft moan of protest whispered from her lips.

"Please," she moaned.

"Yes," he agreed. "I am going to please you until all you can think about is how good I make you feel."

Nudging her thighs apart, he resumed the steady

movement of his fingers, this time exerting just a little more pressure as he worked his way down the inside of one leg and up the other. By the time he'd reached the curve of her ass again, she was desperate for him to touch her *there*, where her hungry, needy sex was making silent demands. When she tried wriggling to change her position, he gave that low, sexy laugh that ignited hunger inside her.

"Pleasure can't be rushed," he told her. "You've had a tough, few days. I want to make sure you're completely relaxed in every part of your body."

Her laugh had a hysterical edge. "Relaxed? Fat chance with you waking up every nerve, as you very well know."

"Oh, we aren't even halfway there yet," he told her.

With a gentle motion of his hands, he rolled her panties down past her hips until he could pull them from her legs and toss them to the floor. She didn't know what she expected next, but it wasn't the light touch of his fingers stroking through the crease between the cheeks of her ass. She sucked in a breath as heat flashed through her, and the inner walls of her sex began to thrum with increasing need.

He ran his fingers through the hot channel once, twice, three time before easing them deeper so he could press on the opening there.

Oh, god!

She remembered how easily he could drive her to orgasm just by doing that, his magic fingers bringing every nerve to life. When he eased them back and slid them lower, between her thighs to the opening of her sex, she groaned in a combination of pleasure and frustration. When he stroked her opening with his fingertips, she did her best to clench around them. She could already feel the orgasm beginning to build.

Just when she was ready to scream with frustration, he rolled her over onto her back, straddled her, and leaned forward to place a kiss on her exposed sex.

A spear of heat shot through her, piercing the channel of her sex and waking up every nerve in her body. The fact that Zander slowly parted those lips and took a long, slow lick of the moist flesh only ratcheted up the need even more.

A frustrated laugh whispered from her lips.

"I thought you were supposed to be relaxing me," she told him.

"You sure look a lot more relaxed. And I think I can do even better than this."

He captured one firm nipple with his lips. As he sucked on it, tugging it and scraping it with his lips, the thrumming inside her ratcheted up. She tried to squeeze her legs together as her inner muscles began to pulse, but Zander was kneeling between them, not allowing her any relief.

"Please," she begged as he turned his attention to the other nipple.

"Please what?"

"You know."

"Please relax you more?"

"Yes. Whatever. You know what I want."

He closed his teeth over one nipple and tugged on it. "This? Is this what you want?"

"Yes. More." She grabbed his head and tugged it upward until his mouth was barely an inch from hers. "You know what I like."

That laugh again.

"I haven't forgotten. Glad you haven't, either."

Sliding down between her thighs, he spread the lips of her sex.

"Close your eyes, Robin. Feel, don't think. That's it."

In moments, his very educated tongue was stroking her damp flash, caressing it, waking up any nerves still sleeping. He moved slowly at first, drawing her up the ladder of sensation, then increasing the pace as her inner walls began to throb in response. By the time he slid two fingers inside her hungry flesh, she was close to the peak of release.

Adding a third finger, he began a steady in and out motion, all the while teasing her clit with his teeth.

The orgasm began to roll up from inside her, her inner muscles spasming as he worked her harder and harder. When he slid his other hand down between the cheeks of her ass and pressed the tips of his fingers against her hot opening, that was all it took to send her over the edge. The walls of her sex convulsed, and she pushed against both of his hands, riding his fingers as wave after wave of convulsions rolled over her.

"Oh, oh, oh." The exclamations slid from her mouth as the orgasm went on and on and on until she was sure she had nothing left inside her. But Zander, who knew her body in every detail, knew exactly how to wring one more spasm, one more convulsion from her.

When the last of the orgasm finally faded, Robin lay there limp and wrung out. Zander kissed his way up her body, paying careful attention to every inch of skin.

"I think you might be relaxed now," he teased.

"I think I might be dead and don't know it." She chuckled and studied his face. "Thank you. For this and everything else."

"No thanks necessary. I'll say it again. The biggest mistake I made in my life was letting you walk away from me. I'm not letting it happen again." He brushed a kiss over her lips. "I think that took all the knots out of your system."

"No kidding. I don't think I can move."

"Then I'll carry you to the shower. Then we'll check on Bobby and crawl into bed. An early night will do us both good."

How had she ever walked away from this man? She gave silent thanks that she'd called him when everything fell apart. What they had between them was more than casual, and she wasn't turning her back on it again. She just hoped the load of trouble she was carrying didn't turn out to be more than he wanted to handle.

Chapter Twelve

Zander's cell phone rang just as they were sitting down to breakfast the next morning. Bobby had slept through the night and seemed a little more energetic. Robin, for her part, still felt like a limp noodle, but she was grateful that Zander had found a way to drain some of the tension from her body.

He grabbed his cell from the table and checked the readout.

"It's Gage," he told her. "Maybe he's got some good news for us."

"So fast?"

"I bet he pulled some strings. Let's see. I'll put it on speaker so we can both hear." He punched the button. "Hey, Gage. What's up? Do you have news for us? I've got you on speaker."

"I do. The lab results on Bobby came back a little sooner than I expected."

The doctor's voice was perfectly calm and even, but Robin's stomach started doing flips and her hands shook. She had to swallow twice before she could speak. "Can you tell me what you found out?"

"I'd like to drop by and explain things to you," he told them. "Everything's always better in person."

"What's wrong?" Robin asked. "It has to be something for you to want to see us."

"Let me explain when I get there, okay? See you in

thirty."

Robin was sure it was the longest thirty minutes she'd ever spent. She did her best not to alarm Bobby, and every kind of tragedy imaginable bounced around in her head. She forced herself to sit at the table, drinking her coffee and making sure Bobby ate, but she couldn't help the feeling of dread creeping over her. She was trying to process what she'd just heard.

"Let's go into the living room," Gage told them when he got there. "Do you have something that Bobby can occupy himself with for a bit?"

"Yes. Let me get him set up."

Finally, they were in the living room, and Gage delivered his news.

"Aplastic anemia?" She knew the term but nothing about it. In her mind, it was some dread disease that scared the life out of her.

Gage nodded. "The lab tests were very clear." He leaned forward. "Did you have any idea about this?"

She shook her head, nearly paralyzed by the shock of it.

"None at all. My sister never mentioned it."

And why hadn't she?

"It isn't always that easy to diagnose," Gage told her. "Especially in its early stages. But it's one of the conditions we specialize in treating, so I ran tests for it just in case."

"And I'm so glad you did." Her brain was still swirling.

"How do we handle it?" Zander reached over to take her hand in his. "What kind of treatment will he need?"

"The good news is, while it's a severe condition, there are many ways to handle it."

"Like what? And how complicated is it?"

"Let me tell you a little about the disease first, okay?" Gage launched into an explanation that was both succinct and in terms Robin could understand.

"A number of things can cause it," he told them, "including a virus. The danger of the disease is when the bone marrow quits producing both red and white blood cells and platelets. Yes, it can be treated with certain medications, but because it is a cancer-related disease. Many times, a bone marrow transplant is required to halt the progress."

"A transplant?" Robin began to quake inside. Oh, god.

Cancer! Bone marrow transplant! She chilled at the words, wondering if she would qualify as a donor if a transplant was necessary. Contacting C.D. would put their lives at risk more certainly than any disease.

"Bobby's condition is in the early stages," Gage went on. "That means we have better chances that it will respond to medication. And of course, if the medication doesn't work, as I said, there's been tremendous success with bone marrow transplants."

Finally, she got her voice working again. "So where do we go from here? What's next?"

"There's a great place right here in town where Bobby can get top notch treatment." The doctor handed a slip of paper across the desk to her. "Southwest Texas General has a department that deals with blood disorders, especially in children. Their doctors are top notch."

Robin blanched. "That all sounds expensive. I-I have medical insurance, but I don't know how far…" She paused. "And he's not even listed on it."

Gage looked at Zander, then at her again. "Okay, so

whatever the situation with him is, we can't follow the usual paper trail procedures. Am I right?"

"It won't be a problem," Zander interrupted. "Whatever is needed will be taken care of."

Robin shook her head. "I can't do that. Take money from you."

"And you won't have to," Gage told her. "Please don't worry about that. I'm on staff at the hospital, and the children's clinic is my specialty. I've already called my boss, the head of the pediatric diseases department there to put Bobby into one of the clinical studies he's doing. That will cover whatever your insurance doesn't."

"Clinical studies?" Another term Robin couldn't quite get her mind around.

Gage gave her a reassuring smile. "It's a good thing, believe me. Like other such specialized departments around the country, they are always studying conditions like this and looking for better ways to treat them. When you go through the admitting process for Bobby, they'll answer your questions a lot better than I can. And I'll still be his leading physician, so feel free to call me any time you have any questions at all."

"What happens when we get there? Where do we go?"

"You'll need to go to Patient Registration first," he said. "It's on the main floor just off the lobby. Just give them my name at the intake desk. They're expecting you. They'll take down all your information. Then someone will walk you over to one of the clinic areas, and finally they'll assign him to a room. Because we need to keep him free of any contagious diseases, the floor he'll be on is a secure one. Only approved people can visit, and you will each be given a special badge to wear."

Robin relaxed a fraction. Good. An extra layer of security.

"And then what?" She wanted to know as much in advance as possible. She was trying to contain both her nerves and her fear.

"They'll assign Bobby to a doctor. I'm not sure who just yet, but whoever it is, he'll be very good. And the process will be very simple, I promise." He looked as if he wanted to give Robin a hug. "I'd say don't worry, except that's impossible where our kids are concerned. But all the doctors at Southwest are wonderful, caring people. You'll be in very good hands. But let's get him to Southwest right away and get the process started. They're expecting him."

As soon as Gage left, Robin made sure Bobby was dressed, and she and Zander took him to the garage where his car was parked.

"What's happening, Aunt Robin?" His voice, tinged with anxiety, crept up a notch. "Am I real sick? Will I be okay?"

Robin looked at him and, with sheer force of will, gathered herself and found a smile for him. "Something is making you sick, honey, and we want to find out what it is. Let me see if I can make you understand what's happening."

Zander ushered them both into the car, and moments later, they were sitting inside while Robin explained what was happening as best she could. She didn't want to drag him into the hospital more scared than she already knew he'd be.

As she talked, his little face got paler and paler, if that was possible, and she saw the fright in his eyes.

"But we'll be right there with you every single

minute," she assured him. "Promise."

"Am I gonna die?" A tear formed in the corner of each eye.

"No." Her voice was fierce. "Absolutely not. I promise you that. We're going to a hospital right here in San Antonio, where they know how to fix the disease you have." She pulled him close and hugged him. "You know all those things you said you wanted to do? Places you wanted to go? And as soon as you get better, we're going to do that. We'll get that baseball glove you were talking about. And a ball. And you can see my pathetic attempts at pitching."

Anything, if only he got well.

He was sniffling as she pressed his head to her shoulder and smoothed his hair. "Do you promise I'll get better?"

"You bet. Dr. Hollander said they'll take very, very good care of you at the hospital. You'll see other kids there as sick as you, and they're all getting better."

I hope.

"Will I have to stay there?"

Robin sensed his body tightening. "Probably for a little while. But I'll stay with you as much as they let me."

He gave a shuddering sigh that raced through his entire small frame. "Okay. But don't stop holding my hand."

"That's a deal." She smiled at him with a reassurance she didn't quite feel.

Please, please, please let them make him well.

****

C.D. was on his fifth cup of coffee, wondering if all the caffeine would kill him, when Frank walked into his office.

"Please tell me you have some information," he growled. The fuse on his temper was getting shorter and shorter.

"Yeah, that would make us all feel a lot better. I tell you, C.D., it's the damnedest thing. It's as if she disappeared off the face of the earth."

C.D. frowned. "Excuse me? Did I just hear you right? Everyone leaves a trail somewhere, and this bitch isn't smart enough to hide herself."

"Yeah? Well, she's done it. If she has a cell, it's a burner. If she's working someplace, it's someplace where they pay her off the books. We tracked her to a rental but that was a dead end. They checked the tracker. One minute, it was in Wyoming, the next Missouri with some salesman, and that doesn't track. It's like she had someone wiping away all the information, although how anyone without connections could manage that, I have no idea."

C.D. ground his teeth. "That bitch isn't smart enough to have arranged this kind of disappearing act by herself. She had help. Get on her. Tear her life apart. Find the name of every person she even had coffee with. Check where she worked. She has to have connected with someone somehow. Dig deeper."

"We want to control this, too," Frank said.

"I think we're way past that. Besides, we've put the word out that she's wanted for murder and kidnapping, so it no longer matters how far we reach out. What matters is what we do with the info when we get it."

Frank nodded. "Understood. Playing off the million-dollar rewards has stirred some action. I'll promote it even more."

"I want the name of everyone she's met since she was an infant. Somewhere, somehow, there is someone she was comfortable enough reaching out to who has the connections to make her disappear. And stay that way."

Frank nodded. "I've been over everything, but I'll take another crack at the people where she worked. Someone there has to know something about her personal life, despite the fact they all say they don't."

"Get me something. And when you find her, make sure she's dead before the cops get to her."

"Got it. Listen, I'm as frustrated as you are. I've never run into so many blank walls in all the time I've been doing this."

"Okay, then. Keep me in the loop."

"Are you doing another press conference?" Frank asked. "It couldn't hurt and might shake something loose."

"Yes. Melanie is setting it up right now." He slammed a fist on his desk. "God damn it to fucking hell anyway? Where in the hell is that fucking bitch?"

****

Zander had no trouble finding Southwest Texas General, sitting as it did right on Interstate 10 heading west out of the city. Along with the referral slip, Gage Hollander had given Robin a hospital brochure, which she read through as they drove.

"Gage marked the section of the parking garage we should use," she told him. "The one for patients being admitted. If they decide he has to stay there, they'll give you a parking pass so we can come and go as we need to. They have a special area for it. Although I plan to spend most of my time right there with him."

Zander heard the tension and worry in her voice and

an underlying note of fear. He'd find a way to make sure she got a good night's sleep each night at the condo, even if he had to kidnap her to do it. It was just as important for her to take care of herself as it was to be with Bobby. She'd be no use to anyone if she ran herself into the ground.

"I'm surprised your sister never mentioned anything about this to you," he told her. "It's a pretty critical situation."

"Gage said it can take a while to show up," she reminded him. "And the symptoms are similar to the flu. It's possible no one thought there was a need for further tests."

"Well, we caught it now," he assured her, "and the hospital will put him on a good treatment plan. And here we are."

"Is this it?" Bobby's voice quavered when he asked the question.

"Yes, it is, honey, and some very nice people are going to help make you all better." She reached over the back of the seat to where Bobby was sitting in the car seat Zander had someone get for him. "Do you believe what I tell you?"

"Y-yes, but I wish my mom was here." The boy's voice trembled.

"Me, too, sweetie, but—"

"But at least my dad can't hurt her anymore."

Robin thought how awful that a five-year-old boy had to have these thoughts.

"That's right, sweetie. She's in a safe place. Now, let's concentrate on you for the moment," Robin told him. "That's what your mom would want."

All the way into the hospital and up the elevator to

the floor they'd been sent to, Zander watched Bobby cling to Robin's hand like a lifeline. The worst mistake he'd ever made in his life—and he'd made some horrendous ones—was letting this woman walk out of his life.

It wasn't until he'd relocated to San Antonio and become part of Guardian Security that he realized it. Watching the partners with their wives brought home to him what he could have had with Robin if he hadn't been so stupid. But he was taking every advantage of her reaching out to him in a critical situation and he wasn't letting her go. Not this time, no matter what they had to face.

In the Admitting area was a very kind woman with a slow, warm voice asking for every piece of information about their lives. Robin changed Bobby's last name on the admission forms, thankfully vouched for by Gage, and told the hospital it was her nephew, which is why their last names were different. She managed her way through the family history without giving away any information. They had a momentary glitch when she was asked to produce an insurance card, but then the woman pulled a note from the pile in front of her.

"Oh, right. Dr. Hollander already left the message he's to be part of the clinical trial we're running. I see he referred you. That's as good a recommendation as we need."

Robin was practically vibrating with nerves, hating the fact that there would be any kind of paper trail, new names or not.

"Hospital records are as private as you can get," he murmured in Robin's ear. "Besides, there's no reason for him to look in that direction. We've got it covered."

"I have one question." The woman looked at Robin. "Would you be willing to be tested in case there was need of a bone marrow transplant?"

"Absolutely." She glanced at Bobby, who still clung tightly to her hand, forehead creased in a worried frown. "Zander, why don't you sit down over there with Bobby while I finish up here? There's no need for hm to stand here."

In other words, get him away from the desk where he's liable to hear something he'll ask questions about.

"Got it. Come on, sport. I'm an old man and need to get off my feet."

That at least got a smile from Bobby, who was looking more scared by the moment.

Zander could tell Robin's body was practically vibrating with nerves while the woman made some notes on the forms, and then they were finished. A pleasant young girl who made it impossible not to be cheerful came to lead them to the clinic area. Every place they walked through was filled with people and adults, some obviously returning patients, others new ones feeling the same trepidation as Robin and Bobby.

The sign over the entrance they walked through said Pediatric Blood Disorders. Inside the area, the hospital atmosphere had been softened with bright murals on the walls. A nurse took their folder from their guide, and they were shown into a small examination room.

"The doctor will be here in just a minute," the nurse smiled. "And he'll take very good care of you," she told Bobby. "You'll like him. All our young patients fall in love with him." She looked at Robin and grinned. "Older patients and mommies, too. Meanwhile, let's get your badges taken care of."

Fifteen minutes later, Robin was sitting on one of the two chairs with Bobby on her lap, whispering reassurances to him, when the door opened, and Gage Hollander walked in.

He smiled at them and shook Zander's hand. "Glad you made it okay, and you've got your badges." He knelt in front of Bobby. "Welcome to my place of business."

Seeing Gage, a familiar face, relaxed Bobby at once.

"I knew you were on staff here," Zander said, "but how did I not know this was your specialty?"

Gage shrugged. "Just never came up. The kind of medical attention you've needed from me isn't part of my specialty. I happen to love kids, so I specialize in pediatrics. I've been here at this clinic for ten years now."

"That's how you were able to get him into the clinical trial."

"It is."

Zander sensed the tension running through Robin's body.

"I didn't even ask I was so focused on getting immediate attention for Bobby, but is the paperwork for clinical trials available to the public?"

Gage shook his head. "No, and it's all done as a double blind. It would take an extraordinary hacker to get this information."

"Let me set your mind at ease and assure you that whatever problem you're dealing with, you and Bobby are safe here at Southwest. You won't be the first people to come here with trouble behind you, I promise you."

Robin twisted her hands together. "Even if you don't know what that problem is?"

"Even if," he assured her. "Unfortunately, we have

a number of, let's say, special circumstances, where the fear the families carried had nothing to do with the disease. Our records are secure, and our only goal is to treat our patients the best we can and make them well."

"Thank you." She let out a heavy sigh, holding onto Gage's words as if they were a lifeline.

Zander held onto her hand, rubbing his thumb across the knuckles.

"I understand we barely know each other," Gage told Robin, "but Zander and I are good friends. He helped me in what I might call a sticky situation, so I owe him big time. Now. Let's take a look at this young man and see if we can fix whatever's wrong with him."

The examination was exhaustive, the lab work extensive, and Gage called in two doctors he worked with for consults. But when all was said and done, the news wasn't too good.

In very simple, basic words, he explained to them the details of aplastic anemia in terms Bobby could understand. And in a voice that soothed fears and offered comfort and security.

"Usually, we begin treatment on an outpatient basis," he told them. "That means, Bobby, you'd come in here for treatment but not stay here." He looked at Robin. "But with his onset so sudden and severe, I think he'll do better if I can monitor him on a twenty-four-hour basis."

The panic was back in Bobby's eyes, and he reached for Robin. "So I haveta stay here? In this place? Not even go to the Vanettas?"

Zander crouched down in front of the little boy. "That will help you get better faster, and Aunt Robin can stay here as much as she likes. Right in the room with you." He looked at Gage. "Am I right about that?"

"Absolutely. We've found that, with the younger patients, it does them a world of good if one parent or special relative is with them at all times. We only allow the one on a twenty-four-hour basis, but you can also have friends come visit during the day."

Bobby's chin quivered. "We don't have any friends here." Then his face brightened. "But maybe the Vanettas can come and visit."

Zander nodded. "I'll make sure of it."

Robin watched Bobby's valiant effort to keep the tears from spilling down his cheeks. She hitched herself up onto the examination table next to him and pulled him into her body.

"Dr. Hollander certainly sounds like he knows what he's talking about, right?" Zander could tell she made her voice as soothing as possible and knew it was much calmer than she actually felt. "And now we know I can be right here with you all the time. So how about it? Let's get you well, shall we?"

Gage deftly maneuvered Bobby into a children's playroom where an aide oversaw what was going on so he could talk with Zander and Robin privately. Zander took Robin's hand in his own and gave it a reassuring squeeze.

"We'll start him on a program of cyclosporine and see how he responds," Gage explained. "Then we'll move him into the clinical trial."

"Of course. Whatever you say. I have to believe what you tell me, Gage. Bobby's life is at stake."

"Forgive me for asking, but where are his parents? Are they dead?"

"His mother is, and his father might as well be."

"All right." Gage nodded. "But there may come a time when we need him. You should be prepared for that."

"I'll cross that bridge when I come to it." *Never.*

Oh, Milla, please forgive me. I feel like I've let you down. I'm doing the best. I promise you.

"We'll get through this," Zander promised. "And I'll be with you every minute.

Chapter Thirteen

It was raining in Seattle, an occurrence so common people usually ignored it. Detective Mac Fontaine and FBI Agent Joel Stetler sloshed through puddles to the diner where they'd chosen to meet for coffee. They wanted to compare notes on a case in which they shared jurisdiction—a murder and a kidnapping. Inevitably, the Ellis situation worked its way into the conversation.

"You know," Stetler commented, stirring sweetener into his cup, "I'd still bet my year's salary, meager as it is, that bastard murdered his wife and is still thumbing his nose at us because he got away with it. I thought that right from the beginning."

Fontaine nodded. "Captain Davis still bitches about how easily the clues leading to the sister-in-law seemed to drop into our laps. And the time we've spent chasing her. He's convinced Ellis manufactured that whole red herring trail. If the evidence was faked, he did a good job of it."

Stetler put down his spoon and sipped at the hot liquid. "If you remember, he was the only one banging the drum about rivalry between the sisters and Robin Fletcher's supposed jealousy. The people we questioned who knew them said the two women were very close, although Ellis didn't allow them to see much of each other." He shook his head. "But they all said Fletcher loved her sister and wanted to get her away from an abusive marriage."

Fontaine grunted. "According to Ellis, he and his wife were the original lovebirds. We couldn't get anyone in the household or his so-called entourage to contradict him."

"Would you have expected less? He's got them by the throat and their pocketbooks."

"Money talks." He shoved his mug away from him. "I just wish she hadn't disappeared the way she did. We didn't even have a chance to question her. And now there's not a trace of her to be found anywhere."

"Well." Stetler drained the last of his coffee. "If she's not the bad guy in all this, I can't say I blame her. Let's say she somehow saw what went on and got the kid out of there. C.D. won't rest until someone brings him her head on a platter."

"That means you big bad feds have to find her first," Fontaine grinned.

"Wouldn't *that* be nice."

Fontaine cocked an eyebrow. "So what's the status with you on the kidnapping charges?"

"I can't make them go away until the kid is found and we know exactly what happened." He shrugged. "The U.S. Marshals are still chasing her down. My boss got her moved up on their 'catch' list, but that's just protocol. And we are definitely keeping an eye on the infamous Mr. Ellis, hoping his ego will cause him to slip up."

"Us, too. Stranger things have happened, and murder is still murder. I have no intention of letting this hit the cold case division." He crumpled his napkin. "Maybe it's time to pay a little visit to the arrogant Mr. Ellis again."

Stetler raised an eyebrow. "You think we'll get anything we haven't already heard from him?"

Fontaine rubbed a hand over his jaw. "I don't know. I just get a weird itch about him. I don't see the anguish and impatience that I'm used to from parents in a situation like this. You know, his performance the day of the funeral was so phony but good, I wanted to give him an award."

"Don't forget. This guy coaches criminals how to act to beat the system. Well, it wouldn't hurt to rattle his cage a little, I guess."

Fontaine stood up and tossed some money on the table. "This one's on me."

"You're all heart," Stetler grinned. "Next time, I suppose you'll want to meet over a steak dinner."

Fontaine just grinned as they headed for the parking lot.

C.D. Ellis was marginally civil to the two law enforcement officers who barged into his office.

"Well," he greeted them, his face expressionless, "if it isn't the Bobbsey Twins come to call. I have appointments to keep, gentlemen, and cases I'm working on. I hope you've come here with news and not just to waste my time."

"We'll just need a minute or two if you don't mind," Stetler told him in a soothing voice.

"Do you have word of my son?" he snapped. "That's the only reason I can think of for you to even show up here."

Fontaine took the lead. "Mr. Ellis, we want nothing more than to find your son, but there's also the question of your wife's murder. Who would kill her and steal the child? Do you really think her sister would do something like that? There has to be more to this. We've been months without a lead here of any kind. We're hoping maybe there's a tiny piece of information you might have forgotten that could help us."

"If you have no results, I'd say you aren't doing your job very well." Arrogance glittered in his eyes. "Maybe I need to put more pressure on your bosses."

Both men knew Ellis had called and tried to throw his weight around with both the Seattle PD and the regional FBI office. With suspicion continuing to grow in everyone's mind, those calls had become a joke.

"What we're hoping for," Stetler continued smoothly, "is something that would give us a clue as to where Robin Fletcher might have taken your son. We've come up dry."

"I don't know what I can tell you." His voice and attitude were barely civil. "The women had no family that I know of. Their parents died in a plane crash several years ago, and there were no other siblings."

"What about cousins?" Fontaine asked. "Aunts or uncles?"

"Gentlemen." Ellis spread his hands out, palms up. "If I knew of such people, wouldn't I have already told you? Why would I keep such information to myself? With my wife dead, my son is the most precious thing in my life. I would do anything to get him back."

Mac already knew there was no other family. He and Joel, separately, had done deep background checks on the women and compared notes. However, they wanted to see what kind of song and dance Ellis would put on for them.

"We're just at a loss for leads," Mac told him, the right note of apology in his voice. "With no ransom demand or other contact, we've finally concluded you're probably right. It's not one of your enemies, so that leaves only your sister-in-law."

"Which I told you from the beginning," he spat at them. The veneer was wearing thin.

"Yes, sir, you did. But we had to follow other possible answers, too. We've now had her put on the U.S. Marshal's fugitive list. Keep in mind, if they find her and she resists arrest, it could end badly for her."

It was evident to both men that if Robin Fletcher ended up dead, Ellis would be very relieved, no matter how hard he tried to conceal it.

"I want my son back," he told them. "What happens to Robin matters little to me as long as she's punished."

"Could you take us through that night one more time?" Stetler asked. "We know it's painful for you, but there may be something you've forgotten."

"I forgot nothing," he snapped, "and I think I've given you as much time as I'm going to. Find my son. Then we'll have something to talk about."

Fontaine and Stetler waited until they were in the parking lot before they spoke.

"He did it," Mac said. "I feel it in my gut."

Joel Stetler nodded. "I agree. And I don't think he wants the kid back because he loves him so much, either. The people who know him said he's obsessed with an heir to carry on his name. And while all this fatherly concern looks good in the media. I can tell he's beginning to fray around the edges, though. Maybe we need to give him another little push."

Mac shook his head. "No, I think he's onto us. We need to pray for a break."

"I'm not much at praying," Stetler told him, "but I'll

do whatever it takes to resolve this thing. You want my honest opinion? I'm damned worried."

"About?"

"What will happen if Ellis finds the woman and the boy before we do? We'll get a live little boy and a dead Robin Fletcher."

"Then we better get our asses in gear."

"Maybe I should think more about praying."

****

Robin was grateful that Gage managed to wrangle a private room for Bobby so she would feel more comfortable as well as Zander. They were both very grateful for it, Zander especially. His relationship with Robin was still in the formative stages, and he wanted things to be as comfortable for her as possible. But he also wanted her to know that he was here for the long haul and whatever Bobby needed, he'd provide what he could. When she took Bobby's hand to give him a reassuring squeeze as they were ushered into what would be his room, Zander took the other hand. He wanted Bobby to know he was there for him, too.

He wished he could find a way to wipe the pinched look from Robin's face. He knew she was doing her best not to show her distress to Bobby. It was obvious, though, that with everything that had happened and this latest development, she was living on the edge of her nerves and this was threatening to be the last straw.

"I was thinking," he told her, once they had Bobby in his room, "what if I run out to the mall we passed and pick up some pajamas for Bobby and get him some toys to occupy himself here? Make him feel not so much like he's in a hospital. There's a huge playroom on this floor, but I'm sure he'd like some things of his own. I peeked in some doors on the way here, and other kids have personal things, too."

"You're right." She nibbled her bottom lip, looking at Bobby with a worried expression. He was digging through the welcome kit the aide had given him when she got him settled in his room. "I'm just not sure about leaving him even for a minute."

Zander took her arm and led her into the hallway.

"Listen. I know you're beside yourself with worry, but like Gage told you, Bobby's going to get the best care here he could get anywhere in the world. That's what Southwest Texas General is all about. It's that way for all of its patients. Everyone who works here is selected with that goal in mind. Even the volunteers." He studied her face, trying to read the expression in her eyes. "I know you're worried about his condition, but that's not all, is it?"

She shook her head. "I'm still afraid somehow this has created a paper trail that C.D. can follow and he'll find us."

"Robin, anything is possible, but that possibility really is remote. And if we get even the hint of it, Guardian is ready to jump in and do whatever has to be done. I promise you nothing will happen to either of you. Take that to the bank. Okay?"

She relaxed against him, although her body still vibrated with tension. "I appreciate what you're trying to do, Zander. More than I ever expected when I called you."

"Then let yourself relax a little and focus on Bobby. He needs you to be calm for him while he goes through this process, which has to be scaring the shit out of him. And all this tension is liable to affect his recovery process. Have you thought about that?"

They stood in silence for a moment. The desperate look in her eyes was destroying him. What he really wanted to do was pull her into a corner away from prying eyes, wrap his arms around her, and kiss away the desperation. Infuse her with his strength. Let her know he was there for her. And not just for a day or two. He was definitely in it for the long haul.

Bobby looked up when they walked through the door. He was obviously putting on his brave face, but unshed tears clouded his eyes.

"Can you get me the airplane pajamas you bought me?" he asked. "Will they let me wear them here? They make me feel really good."

She pulled him into her arms and hugged him tightly.

"How about if I get you a new pair and some things to play with? That work for you? Zander said he's up for some shopping."

"But when will you do that?"

Robin knew the whiny edge to his voice was due to the stress of the day's activities and the shock of his illness.

"I'm leaving right now to get them," Zander answered. "And maybe some surprises.

"But—"

Robin motioned him to step out into the hall with her again.

"Don't leave," Bobby cried out. "Where are you going now?"

"I'm only going out in the hall for a moment," she assured him. "I'll be right back. Promise." She turned to Zander. "Not that I don't appreciate every single thing you are doing, especially just jumping into my situation the way you are. But I know you must have work obligations. Things to take care of. Zander, you are going way above and beyond anything I expected."

He cupped her face in his hands, his palms warm against her cheeks.

"This *is* my work obligation. Personal feelings aside, you are my client, and as I always do, I am devoting one hundred percent of my attention to you." He winked. "And let me tell you, I'm enjoying it a lot more than my other clients."

"I—just feel so guilty."

"Robin." His tone was very serious now. "I'll do anything to keep you safe and protect you, but it's also personal for me, and I hope you know that. Whatever fates conspired to throw us together again after all this time, I'm going to take full advantage of it. And if you and Bobby didn't get one hundred percent of my attention, I shouldn't be doing this."

She stared into his eyes as if trying to read a message there. "What did I ever do to deserve you?"

He grinned. "I'm sure I can think of plenty of ways for you to repay me." He brushed his mouth over hers. "Meanwhile, let's get Bobby taken care of so he feels more comfortable in this situation. He has to be scared to death, and he's probably freaking with us walking in and out of the room."

"Thank you. For everything."

Zander was just getting ready to leave when Gage walked in with a tall man who looked to be about sixty years old. Lean and muscular, with short cut iron gray hair, he had startling blue eyes that, right now, had a twinkle in them for Bobby.

"This is Jim Mercer," Gage told her. "He's one of our special volunteers who come here to work with the kids. They all call him Grandpa."

"Hey, Bobby." Jim Mercer walked over to the bed and held out his hand. "I'm very pleased to meet you."

"Me, too." Bobby shook hands solemnly, then glanced over at Robin, telegraphing, *Who is this man?*

Gage motioned Robin and Zander to the side.

"Jim's a retired cop who spends most of his time here with the kids. He's been a volunteer for five years. I don't know what kind of trouble you're dealing with, but I wanted to help. I'd feel safe leaving my own kids with him if I had any."

"Thank you so much." Robin felt some of the tension drain from her. "I appreciate it. If you only knew…"

He held up a hand. "And I don't need to."

Robin had to swallow back tears. In her wildest dreams, when she left Seattle, she'd never imagined the reception she'd get from Zander and everything that now was part of that. If only the police could get the proof they needed against C.D., she could think about living something close to a normal life. With Bobby. And Zander. Definitely with Zander…if he didn't decide this was more than he bargained for.

While Zander was gone, a nurse came in to give Bobby his first shot of cyclosporine, and shortly after that, he dozed off. Robin sat next to the bed for a long time, touching his hair, his face, his arms, as if her hands could wipe away the disease that had invaded his body. Just when she thought things had settled down for them, Fate decided for whatever reason to give them a kick in the ass.

But I have Zander. Thank god. And Guardian Security.

What more could she ask for in the turmoil swirling around them?

Chapter Fourteen

The first night at the hospital was tense for all of them, but Robin finally got Bobby to sleep, and she and Zander left to go home. She was on edge every moment during the first couple of days of the cyclosporin treatment. The nurses and Gage had been great about explaining to Bobby everything that was happening and calming his distress. Robin thanked Zander over and over again for hooking her up with Gage Hollander and the subsequent connection to the hospital.

And Zander. What a godsend. He was so good with Bobby, she wanted to cry. He'd bought some books so the two of them could read together and some board games they could play. Bobby wasn't confined to the room, so they took some walks in the hall with him and also spent some time in the playroom at the end of the hall. Robin had hoped Bobby would make friends with some of the children who spent time there, but he didn't seem to feel comfortable with anyone but her and Zander.

Guardian was keeping tabs on the story of Milla's murder and Bobby's disappearance, monitoring all the electronic news channels. Zander told her they'd made contact with one of the police in Seattle who was working the case, a Seattle detective named Fontaine. Zander knew the man had checked out Guardian in minute detail before sharing information with him. But both Reno Sullivan and Nick Vanetta had been part of cases that involved the FBI, so their credentials more than passed scrutiny.

But Zander also checked his computer daily for stories about Milla's death and Bobby's disappearance.

"Even with the million-dollar bounties," he told Robin, "the story has become localized. Too much other news that's taking precedence."

"Thank the lord for that," she told him. "Since I don't plan for us ever to go back to Seattle, maybe this will all die down and I can figure out how to create a new life for Bobby and me."

Zander looked at her, something hot and deep swirling in his eyes. "One, the cops aren't going to just let this die a natural death, if you'll excuse the pun. And two, I sort of had it in mind that whatever new life you create was built around the three of us. Or am I misreading signals here?"

She took a moment to answer him. "I want that, too. But this is always going to be hanging over our heads if we don't find evidence that C.D. killed Milla. I wasn't sure you were up for living a life where you always have to look over your shoulder."

Zander took her hand in his. "I'm in this for the long haul, Robin. And we will make sure C.D. doesn't get away with this. Then the three of us can build a future. Together."

They were words she clung to as she worried about their situation and Bobby's future.

Zander checked in with the office regularly to see if there was anything new or they had any questions for Robin. Guardian was using all its resources to find a thread to pull, but so far no luck. But Bobby was settling a little more into the routine. Lindsey Vanetta had come to visit, something that cheered Bobby up a great deal. And Jim Mercer dropped by each day at lunchtime so Robin and Zander could take a little break. Robin was thrilled to see how Bobby connected with the older man. With her parents deceased, there was a whole generation missing. Sometimes, she wondered, if her parents hadn't been killed in the plane crash, would Milla still have married C.D.? He swept into her life at a critical time and in the beginning filled a need.

Zander and Detective Fontaine both agreed they were missing something, but C.D. Ellis was so used to camouflaging what he did that they couldn't figure out what.

"There's no thread to pull," he told Robin, "but count on this. We're not giving up. Sooner or later, he'll make a mistake and we'll get him."

"I'm just glad the story has hardly made it into the media here," Robin told him. "If one of the nurses or anyone else here at the hospital saw his picture, we'd be in big trouble."

"There's been too much news pushing it to the back. Let's hope it stays that way."

Fontaine had told them it was still big news in Seattle, and every couple of days someone would write a story with a headline asking for information on Bobby Ellis or Robin Fletcher. It seemed, however, that while the million-dollar bounties had generated what Zander called a shitload of responses, none of them had an accurate information.

Bobby had been on the cyclosporine for nearly a week now. She worried that the little boy's color didn't improve. That his nausea seemed to come and go with greater frequency. That he seemed to be more fatigued than ever and he napped twice a day now rather than his usual once. And as much as she tried to convince herself she was imagining things, she could tell that Gage wasn't as pleased with Bobby's progress as he wanted to be.

Still, he tried to soften her fears.

"Let's not panic until we have to, okay?" he told her. "I'm watching him closely. If I need to make a change in his treatment, I'll tell you why and we'll discuss all the options."

"Exactly how many options are there?" She was back to chewing on her lips again.

"Each patient is different," he pointed out. "Please don't panic until you have to, okay? It's important for Bobby that he see you calm and confident about his progress."

But panic wasn't something she could just wish away, and it nagged at her constantly. And at night, when she lay in Zander's arms, she wondered if they'd ever catch a break.

She was amazed at the number and breadth of activities Southwest offered its young patients being treated for catastrophic diseases. Every effort was made to divert children's minds from the intensity of their illness and the seriousness of the situation. Even the outpatients were encouraged to participate.

Robin tried to blank the word catastrophic from her mind and concentrate simply on Bobby and projecting his recovery. She couldn't allow herself to think in any other way.

One afternoon, Gage came into Bobby's room with a very pretty blonde, round and petite with warm hazel eyes.

"Meet my sister Tracy," he said. "She's a child psychologist, and she's on the staff here. I want her to make the connection with Bobby because there might be a situation where she's needed. Especially when we get through this and he thinks about his mother even more."

Robin smiled and shook the woman's hand. His sister? Was she a doctor, too?

Tracy held out her hand. "Hi! Nice to meet you."

"Likewise." Robin frowned. "Do you usually visit his patients?"

She nodded. "In a lot of cases where Gage thinks I can be a help. This is a stressful situation, and sometimes it helps to talk to a professional who can give you hints on how to deal with it. I'm leaving my phone number with you, just in case you get the urge. Call any time." She handed Robin a slip of paper.

Robin blinked back tears. "I don't know what to say."

"Just say you'll call." She moved closer to the bed. "The other reason I'm here is to take this young man to Puppet Time."

"Tracy coordinates a puppet show for the kids once a week," Gage explained. "I thought Bobby would enjoy it."

"Can I, Aunt Robin?" Despite the fact that she and Zander had taken him to the playroom when he felt up to it and to a couple of movies on the big screen television, the puppet show seemed to strike a spark. His eyes showed the first spark of life since the day of their initial visit to the hospital.

"As long as Xander and I are with you."

"Of course." Tracy smiled. "Family enjoys it as much as the kids."

The afternoon was very pleasant, and Tracy was wonderful to be with. She went out of her way to make Robin and Zander feel at ease, introducing them to some of the other parents. At first, Bobby practically plastered himself to her side, but as the puppet show progressed and the puppeteer called on the different children to participate, he seemed to relax more. He even crawled into Zander's lap while he watched.

When the puppet show ended and they were back in Bobby's room, a nurse came in to give him his scheduled dose of medication.

A look of distress flashed over Bobby's face.

"How many times do they have to do this?" he asked. "And when can I go home?"

Robin wondered exactly where he was referring to when he said home. She still hadn't figured out how to tell him they were never going back to Seattle.

"That depends on what the tests they keep taking show. I promise we want to get you out of here as soon as possible, but we want you to be healthy when we do."

That seemed to satisfy him for the moment, but she knew it wouldn't last.

By the end of Bobby's second week in the hospital, he seemed to be accepting his situation, but Robin was a wreck. Each day, she tensed when they administered his meds and she questioned the nurse about his vitals and any changes at all. The fact they told her every patient was different didn't help at all. Keeping a calm exterior for her nephew took everything she had. If not for Zander, she was sure she would have lost her mind.

"Gage said the treatment is working," Zander reminded her one night after they arrived home after another day that exhausted her. "And Bobby's become a real trooper."

"Because the hospital gears everything toward making the kids secure and not frightened. And thank goodness for that."

"I think a glass of wine is called for," he told her, "so we can make sure you feel secure and not frightened." His fingers kneaded her shoulders. "Your muscles are so tight, it's a wonder they haven't snapped."

"Wine would be nice," she agreed,

Zander poured two glasses, handed one to her, and touched his glass to hers. "To success all around. Bobby's health, the truth about Milla's murder, and a long prison sentence for C.D. Ellis."

"I'll drink to that," she agreed. When they'd finished their wine, she rose from the couch. "I think I need a long, hot shower."

"I agree. Get some of that tension out of your body."

In her bedroom, she stripped off her clothes, then walked into the en suite bathroom and turned on the shower. When it was as hot as she could stand it, she stepped into the enclosure and let the hot stream pour over her body. It felt so good to just stand there and let the heat pound away at the tension in her muscles.

Once again, she sent up a little prayer of thanks that Zander had welcomed her with open arms and without questions. She really had no other options. She grabbed the bottle of body wash sitting on a little recessed shelf and poured a generous portion into her hand. But when she began to apply it to her skin, the shower door opened, Zander stepped in and scooped the thick liquid from her hand.

"I think this is my job," he told her, his voice low

and deep, vibrating at her ear.

In seconds, his hard, naked body was pressed against hers, his thick cock nestled in the crease of her ass, his large hand working the body wash into her tense muscles.

"Close your eyes," he murmured, his mouth close to her ear. "Don't think. Just feel."

She knew it was selfish of her, but god, she needed this so badly. Zander could make her feel things no one else ever had or ever could. And he asked nothing in return. So she stood there while he worked the slick liquid into her muscles, kneading them with his fingers. Shoulders first, then her upper arms, then down the length of her back. When he reached the cheeks of her ass and he rubbed the thick wash into the skin, kneading the cheeks, a shiver raced over her.

But her senses really cried out when he slid two soapy fingers into the hot crease and rubbed them up and down.

"Ooohhh." The little moan escaped her lips all on its own.

"Feel good, baby?" His mouth was right at her ear, and he nipped the lobe gently.

"You know it," she told him. "Sinfully so."

He crouched down to work on her legs, his fingers brushing the lips of her sex when he massaged her inner thighs. Until she and Zander had reconnected, she had forgotten what it felt like to have a man make love to her, especially this man. Making love with him was beyond imagining. Beyond description. *This* didn't just make her body sing; it reached into her heart.

Zander made every other lover she'd had fade into insignificance. He touched her as if she was a prized treasure, caressed her like something precious.

He went to work with meticulous care on the front of her body, cupping her breasts and kneading them while he lightly pinched her nipples. She felt the sensation through her entire body and tried to squeeze her legs together against the tiny spasms that were pinging in her sex.

But Zander would have none of it. He nudged her legs apart, found her clit, and pinched and tugged it until she was sure she'd come just standing there.

When his mouth covered hers again, she felt the kiss all the way to her toes and every other part of her body. It was both taking and giving, plundering and soothing, the most emotional kiss they'd shared yet. His tongue swept inside with the softness of a caress and the lick of a flame. His large hands slid up her body and cradled her head, holding it to him as he drank his fill.

Can you worship someone's mouth? To Robin, that's what it felt like. A kiss of almost reverent proportions. She felt every pulse in her body leap to life and liquid seep from her hot, moist center. She heard a moan drift through the air and realized it was hers. Her arms slipped beneath his and wrapped around him, feeling the hard, sleek muscles of his back.

His cock pressed against her, hard and hot. She reached down for it, wanting to wrap her fingers around the velvety skin. He circled her wrist with his fingers and gently moved her hand away.

"Feel how ready I am?" he groaned. "I don't want to embarrass myself and come to the party before it's time." He nipped her ear lobe. "I want this to last, okay?"

Before she could answer, he moved one of his hands down the slope of her shoulder and over to her breasts, cradling one as his thumb chafed her nipple. It immediately beaded, leaping to life, a shock of pleasure streaking straight to her core. He lowered his head to catch her other nipple with his rough velvet lips, and Robin thought she would explode.

He teased and played with her nipples, kneading her breasts with his warm, capable hands, until she was ready to scream.

More, more, more.

His tongue traced patterns along the upper slope of her breasts and in the valley between them. Sometimes, he nipped with his teeth, very, very gently, then soothed with his tongue. She'd never realized exactly how turned on this made her. But then, no one had ever worshiped her breasts the way Zander was doing.

Of all the sex they'd had, nothing compared to this.

When one of his hands slid smoothly down her abdomen to brush the damp curls at the apex of her thighs, her legs shifted apart again.

Yes, she wanted to scream. *Inside me.* But she couldn't make her mouth work.

As he'd teased and played with her breasts, now he did the same with the curls covering her sex and the length of her cleft. And all the while, he spoke softly in her ear, alternating gentle licks of his tongue with soft, sexy words.

"Your skin is like satin, Robin. So smooth. And your breasts, so warm in my hands with nipples like plump strawberries. I could suck on them all night long and never be satisfied."

He shifted slightly, tangling his fingers in her pubic curls. "Just like coils of silk," he whispered. "I want to touch them forever, feel the dampness of your arousal on them, suckle your breasts while your liquid heat flows into my hand."

His fingers parted her folds as if he were opening the petals of a flower, spreading the skin to touch the slickness hidden inside. The glide of his finger into her tight channel was like the flame of a torch, setting every nerve in her body on fire. She felt herself flutter and quiver around his fingers even as tiny spasms raced through her. Her body was not her own but merely his to do with as he wished.

"I want to taste you," he murmured, his voice low and thick.

She opened her legs in invitation, waiting with breathless anticipation as he kissed his way down the flatness of her abdomen, pausing only to tease at her navel and swipe at her curls with the tip of his tongue.

His hands and mouth were everywhere, exploring the crease of thigh and hip, the sensitive bend of the elbow, the tender skin of inner thigh. His tongue was like a torch, lighting a flame wherever it touched her.

And then he was there, his head between her legs, his thumbs opening her to his eyes and his mouth.

"Bend your legs," he whispered.

When she did, he licked her everywhere, tasting her, probing her, his mouth pulling at the tight, erogenous knot that begged for attention. She was hot, her breathing erratic, her heart thundering, and a tight spiral of need slowly unwound low inside her. He shifted his hands and slid them beneath her bottom, pulling her toward his mouth for greater access. A low, keening sound erupted from her as every nerve screamed in answer to the myriad of sensations.

"You smell like sweet peaches and taste like pure

honey. I don't think I'll ever get enough of tasting you. Ever."

He suddenly stopped, and she wanted to scream and pull at his hair, push his head back where he'd been doing such wonderful things to her. The sound of the shower door opening startled her, but then she heard it close again, heard the tearing of foil and glanced down to see Zander sheathing himself.

And then he was there, between her quivering thighs, rubbing his pulsing shaft at her opening, slowly, agonizingly slowly, moving inside her until he filled her completely.

Robin thought she'd died and gone to heaven. The feel of him was beyond description. She clamped her internal muscles around him, holding him tightly even as he stretched her unbelievably.

"Look at me, Robin. Open your eyes and look at me."

Her eyelids felt thick and heavy, but she forced them open and saw his eyes blazing into hers.

"Keep looking at me. That's it. God, I can see clear into your soul."

And then he was moving within her, slowly at first, steady, then faster. As he increased the tempo, she matched the rhythm, moving with him, thrusting her hips at him. He rocked against her, holding her gaze with eyes that mesmerized her.

She felt it beginning, gathering inside her, the slow climb up the spiral, muscles gathering and pulsating, moving from low in her belly to spread throughout her body. When her nails dug into the skin of his back and her legs tightened around him, when her breath came quicker and harder, he thrust hard and strong.

"Now, Robin," he gasped. "Come with me now."

She bathed him in her hot liquid heat as she splintered and flew in tiny pieces, whirling into the blackness. Spasms racked her harder and harder, and she felt him pulsing inside her. She was afraid it would never stop. She never wanted it to stop. She flew to a place she'd never reached before and in the final, shuddering movement of their bodies, she knew she was his.

He turned off the shower and lifted her out onto the bathmat, then wrapped her in a towel warm from the heated towel bars. After he dried them both off, he lifted her and carried her into the bedroom, then yanked back the covers and placed her on the sheets. When he was lying next to her, he wrapped his arms around her and tucked her head to his shoulder.

"I'll say this as many times as I need to. We're in this together, Robin. For the long haul. I've never told another woman I love her, but I'm saying it to you. I love you. We're going to clean up this mess and start a new life as a family, you and me and Bobby. You can take that to the bank."

For the first time, she began to believe that would actually happen.

Chapter Fifteen

Robin felt refreshed and calmer the next day—thanks to Zander—until Gage came in that afternoon. He had a more than usual serious look on his face as he motioned them into the hall. "Let's chat in my office for a few minutes. Okay?"

All her calm disappeared at once. "Something's wrong."

"Let's just say I have some concerns. Come on. My office is a better place to chat."

She and Zander made sure Bobby was occupied and distracted before following Gage. When they were settled in two chairs by his desk, he opened a folder and looked at its contents.

"I've just looked at this morning's lab results," he told them, "and I think we need to take a hard look at Bobby's situation."

She felt nausea rising in her throat and swallowed hard. "He's worse, isn't he?"

"Not necessarily," he corrected, "but there are some changes I'm not all that happy with. He's not at a crisis stage yet, but the medication isn't working the way I'd hoped and the disease is progressing."

"W-What can we do?" The terror she'd been trying to ignore grabbed her hard, and she reached for Zander's hand.

"There are some other things we can try, but…"

"But?"

"But we may have to face the fact that our only answer is a bone marrow transplant."

Icy cold fingers ran down her spine. Dear lord.

"Test me," she said at once. "I asked about that in the very beginning, and I want to do it right now."

Gage nodded. "Absolutely. We'll do it tomorrow. I was going to suggest it, anyway. But what if you're not a match? Sometimes even parents aren't."

"But other members of the family could be?"

"It's our next choice if the parents aren't compatible. Or in this case, aren't available. The medical history you gave us is sketchy at best and doesn't give us a lot of options. I know you said his mother is dead but what about the father? Would he donate?"

Robin gave a vehement shake of her head. "Not in the picture and cannot be contacted. Not under any circumstances."

She wanted to curl into a ball and pretend this whole thing wasn't happening. She wasn't going to reach out to C.D. who would kill her and snatch Bobby. He had the manpower to do it.

"What about a system like you have for organ transplants?" she asked. "Don't they have one for bone marrow, too?"

He nodded. "We can enter Bobby's name in it if you aren't a match, but there may be a lot of people ahead of him."

"Oh." She chewed on her bottom lip.

"The other thing we can do is put out a call for volunteers to be tested. We do that all the time, too."

"No." She nearly shouted the word, then forced herself to be calm. "I don't want that kind of publicity surrounding him."

Gage cocked his head and studied her face. Then he nodded. "Okay, no big publicity. I assume the reason for that is whatever baggage you're carrying. No problem. We can do it within the hospital, and we have a volunteer system we can use. The whole thing would be very contained. I just don't want to be in a position where we're gambling with his life."

The tears spilled over again before she could stop them. Zander moved next to her, pulled out his handkerchief, and blotted her tears. He held her as she pressed her face to his shoulder, her tears soaking his shirt as she cried in silence. No more making a spectacle of herself. Finally, she was cried out, her eyes and throat raw, her chest tight.

"This has to stop," Zander said softly. "You're making yourself sick, and you won't be any good to Bobby."

"I know, I know." She inhaled a deep, shuddering breath.

He looked at Zander. "Is there something you can clue me in on so I don't make a mistake?"

Zander looked at Robin, who nodded.

"Okay," he said. "I can tell you that these two are in terrible danger. If I tell you what it is, it could make the danger worse."

Gage frowned. "We've faced dangerous situation many times, especially patching up people who needed to disappear. Is this the same kind of thing?"

"Pretty much. Robin has gone through a lot to keep Bobby safe. We can't change things now, and we don't want to put you in jeopardy, too."

"I appreciate it," he told them, "but I think you know

I can handle it. And depend on you to keep the danger away from both Bobby and me. And I'm guessing the danger has something to do with Bobby's father."

"Yes." Robin shook her head.

"All right." He looked at Zander. "I'll depend on you and Guardian Security to keep us protected. It's one of the things you do best. But if the tests tomorrow don't show that you're a match, we have to take the next steps. And I'll see if there's a way to get Bobby on the lists without using his name. I'm pretty sure it's been done before for high level patients."

"Thank you." Robin breathed a sigh of relief. "Keeping him hidden is a top priority."

Outside Bobby's room, Zander stopped and pulled her into his arms. "We'll keep you and Bobby hidden no matter what we have to do. And make sure he gets what he needs medically to be a thriving, healthy little boy."

"I'll never be able to thank you enough."

"Oh. I think I can find a way." He brushed a kiss over her lips. "Now let's get back to our boy."

Our boy.

She liked the sound of that.

****

"You're taking the Delaware case?" Frank asked, watching C.D. finish making notes on his laptop.

"Yes." Ellis saved the document and opened a new one. "For what he's paying me, I'd be nuts to turn him down." You'll have to go to San Antonio, though, and you have no idea how long you'll be there."

Ellis looked up at Frank with narrowed eyes. "Is there some reason you don't think I should go, Frank? If so, spit it out."

Frank shrugged. "No big deal. It's just...well...the

case on your wife's death is still open, and the cops might think it's weird that you defend another man accused of killing his wife."

Ellis closed out his work, shut down the laptop, and sat back in his chair. When he spoke, his sarcasm slashed like a knife. "How considerate of you to think of that. Are you saying that I'm a suspect in Milla's death? And if I defend Jason Delaware, they'll see it as like goes to like?"

Frank spread out his hands. "I'm just saying."

"First of all, let me remind you I was never, ever accused. Of anything. They tried damned hard but couldn't get anywhere. Still can't. The cops have no evidence, and those in our pocket managed to dilute or get rid of what there was. Secondly, if they truly think I killed my wife, what do they think I did with my son? Kill him, too?"

"But boss, you know—"

"I know there's nothing that points to me and Bobby is still missing. And finally, I'm a criminal defense attorney, and that's what I'm expected to do. Defend criminals. This isn't the first time I've taken an out-of-town case, and I'm sure it won't be the last." He snorted. "There are only so many rich criminals in Washington."

"Okay, okay." Frank backed off. "You always tell me to say what I think. That's all I'm doing."

"If they'd find the damn kid and that bitch of a sister-in-law, all this would go away." He stood up and went to his office window, which had a panoramic view of downtown Seattle. "I'm telling you, Frank. We've taken her life apart one tiny piece at a time, and there isn't one fucking clue as to where she's gone. Or how."

"We hired the best. You know that. If there was

anything to find, they'd have dug it up."

"Well, tell them to keep on digging. Go back to her friends again. Her boss. Her neighbors. Someone saw or heard something at some time. Some incident in her life. We have to find it. And before the cops do."

"When are you planning to leave?"

"Tomorrow morning. Melanie called the pilot to make sure my plane is ready and set up my hotel reservations. I talked with Jason this morning. I'll be meeting with him at four thirty tomorrow afternoon." He made a face. "Unfortunately, this is right at the beginning of their big Fiesta shindig. The crowds will be suffocating. Melanie said she was lucky to get me a suite."

"Are you meeting him at the hotel?"

"Yeah. There's some procession or pilgrimage or whatever and a big deal in front of the Alamo, and he's bitching about the traffic. I told him tough shit. If he wants me to defend him, he can make it convenient for *me*."

"Are you taking your usual security?"

C.D.'s smile was like an icicle. "Would I not? Crowds tend to get abusive, especially in cases like this." He began gathering folders on his desk. "I want regular calls from you on my cell phone. Just because I'm out of town doesn't mean things come to a standstill."

Frank nodded. "Understood. I'll take care of it."

"See that you do."

****

When Robin and Zander arrived at the hospital for the donor tests, she was more nervous

"I have to be a match, Gage." She let out a long slow breath. "I just don't have any other options."

He rubbed her back gently, the way you'd soothe a child. "That's not exactly true, but we'll cross that bridge when we come to it. Just remember that Bobby's the important thing here. We have to do whatever we can to make sure he's well."

"And safe." She sniffled. "It won't do him much good to be cured if…" She shook her head and scrubbed her hands across her face. "Let me just wash my face, and I'm ready."

She made sure Bobby was occupied. One of the volunteers took him to the playroom where he'd be occupied for quite a while. Then Gage took her and Zander down to the lab where Zander held her hand while they did the testing.

"Aren't you supposed to be working?" she asked Gage at one point.

"I am," he grinned. "I'm doing things for my patient."

"But you must have other patients who need your attention. And the clinic. I don't want to take you away from them."

"You're not. Besides, I owe Zander a debt I might never be able to repay. A little of my time is just a small down payment."

"Oh, Gage." Tears threatened again. She felt like a leaky hose. "You don't know how much…how I…"

He smiled. "I know. And we will get this fixed. Everything," he stressed, and she knew what he meant.

When she was finished giving blood, he walked with her and Zander back to Bobby's room. He was back from the playroom, and the nurse was there, administering another dose of the medicine.

"We'll keep him on this until we know what our

next move is," Gage told them.

Robin's heart fractured at the sight of the little boy's brave, pale face. He'd hardly complained, and she knew how scared he must be. Sometimes, when he dozed off, she heard him cry out, and she climbed into bed with him, holding his little body tight against hers and praying harder than she'd ever prayed in her life.

I'm trying, Milla. I'll make him better whatever it takes.

"How goes it, sport?" Zander asked, sitting down beside Bobby.

"Okay," Bobby said in a thin voice. "But I'll sure be glad when I can get out of here."

"That doesn't say a whole lot for our hospitality." Gage grinned. "But I know what you mean."

The little boy turned to look at Robin. "Everyone's talking about this Fiesta thing. I know I can't go, but can you get me a Fiesta T-shirt?"

"Oh, honey. Of course." She sighed. "I'll just have to pick a time to go downtown when the traffic won't kill me."

"Guys, I have a suggestion." Gage came to stand beside the bed. "At four o'clock this afternoon, there's an event that I think is really what this celebration—this city—is all about. All of the genealogy groups, led by the Sons and Daughters of the Republic of Texas, march in a solemn procession to the Alamo where the names of the defenders are read and a special ceremony is held."

"Oh, wow!" Bobby's eyes opened wide. "Like a parade?"

"Only more special," Gage told him. "This is history, kid. This is what Texas is all about."

"It's bound to be jammed downtown, though,"

Robin protested. "I don't even know if we could find a place to park."

"I can take care of that. The Menger Hotel is right across from the Alamo, and the doorman is a former patient. Let me give him a call, and you can park right in front. Just look for Patrick. He should be right outside."

"And I can leave my car there?"

"There are vendor booths set up in the little park right there. Give yourself enough time to get Bobby's T-shirt, take pictures of the event with your cell phone, and then get out while the getting's good."

"Could you, Aunt Robin?" Bobby pleaded.

Zander looked at Gage. "What do you think?"

Gage looked at his watch. "If you leave here about two, you'll have plenty of time to get there, even if the streets are clogged. You want to get to the Alamo before all the places in front are filled."

"Okay. You talked me into it. But you'll call Patrick, right?"

"I'll do it right now. I have two late appointments today, or I'd take you guys myself." He looked at his watch. "But how about this. I should have the information from the lab by that time. Go home after you take the pictures, put on something a little spiffier than usual, and go out for dinner for a change." He winked. "Maybe you'll be celebrating."

"From your lips to God's ear," she said in a fervent voice. "All right. But will Mr. Mercer be able to come earlier to be with Bobby while we're gone?"

Gage nodded. "I'll work it out."

She tried to smile. "Thank you, Gage."

Chapter Sixteen

C.D. was grouchy as a bear with an injured paw when he arrived in San Antonio. The flight had been bumpy, and it interrupted his concentration as he prepared for his meeting with Jason Delaware. At the airport, they'd been kept in a holding pattern for fifteen minutes. Then Fiesta traffic made the trip to the hotel twice as long as he expected. He was only glad he'd required the limo he'd hired to have a fully stocked bar, or he'd have been tearing his hair out. He was not a person who dealt well with adversity, especially these days.

Fortunately, the suite Melanie had reserved and the arrangements she'd ordered more than met his expectations. Two printers and two fax machines were set up, ready to be connected. He'd dictate everything using a voice recognition program, sending it back to his office. His associates and paralegals would prepare what he needed and do the leg work. It meant he didn't have to deal with anyone locally, which he preferred. The fewer people involved in his business, the better.

The welcome basket from the hotel was a nice touch as was the assistant to the concierge who said he could call their desk twenty-four/seven for anything he needed. They paid special attention to special clients.

C.D. thanked him with a hefty tip and immediately opened the minibar. Jason Delaware was a bundle of nerves and would require a lot of handholding. The man didn't mind grinding other people under his heel, but he didn't handle being in the hot seat himself very well.

He'd bitched and complained because C.D. couldn't get there for his arraignment, even though the attorney Ellis sent managed to get him bailed out. Not an easy feat, considering the charge. The guy needed a reality check.

His cell phone rang, and he checked the incoming number. George. One of his two security people.

"You picked up the cars okay?" he asked.

"Got them," George told him.

Melanie always arranged for George and whoever else was with him to have two rental SUVs available whenever they traveled with their boss. Even though C.D. liked the use of a limousine himself, he always insisted his men have a vehicle at the ready wherever he stayed. He never knew when one of them might have to move fast, and this was a prime example.

"Okay. It's jammed to hell downtown here. Give the doorman a hundred bucks and park one of the vehicles at the curb in case we need it. And let's try to keep a lid on the whole thing."

"That might be impossible. The media is dogging your every step, plus you're about to take on a new high-profiled client in the midst of your personal upheaval."

"Damn it." He slammed a fist against a chair."

"I'll do what I can. You know that. See you in a bit."

C.D. poured some Wild Turkey over ice and sat back in one of the easy chairs, sipping at the aged whiskey. He needed to get rid of his own tension so he could be the picture of calm for his client.

****

The traffic slowed down around Zander and Robin about ten minutes before the exit Robin was looking for, but she'd left herself more than enough time. And although they moved slowly, at least they weren't stopped. The going was even slower when they exited the Interstate and moved in fits and starts down Commerce Street to Alamo Plaza.

Patrick, a gangly teenager who took his part-time job very seriously, was waiting for her at the main entrance to the Menger, the historic hotel where Teddy Roosevelt had met to recruit Rough Riders.

"Dr. Hollander said to take good care of you." He gave them both a wide grin. "Just leave everything to me."

"Are you sure it's okay for us just to park here?" She looked around nervously.

"Sure. No problem. Got it covered." He lifted the piece of cardboard he'd been holding in one hand and slid it under her windshield. The letters VIP were printed in heavy black ink.

"Oh, Patrick, I'm not sure"

"I swear it's all right. I do this for people all the time."

"But aren't they usually guests of the hotel?" she asked.

He shrugged. "Well, you might be sometime."

"Okay. Well, we'd better get going if I want to get my nephew his T-shirt and still find a place to watch from."

"We're covered," Zander said. "Gage did a good job setting this up. But let's get moving anyway. We're on a limited time schedule."

He took her hand and led her across the blocked off

street to the front of the Alamo.

"Gage was right about the crowd," she commented. "Wow! I think everyone in San Antonio must be here."

"I Googled it," Zander told her. "This is the celebration for San Antonio. Maybe for all of Texas."

Already, they were jostling each other in the space allowed for spectators. Robin wondered if she'd find a place to watch at all. She managed to take pictures of the setup in front of the Alamo while they searched for a place to stand.

A color guard was in readiness at the side of the entrance and short rows of chairs had been set up to the side of a platform.

"For the Daughters," a man told her when she asked. He looked to be in his sixties and wore a T-shirt that said, "*I don't need to get to heaven. I live in Texas.*"

She frowned. "Excuse me?"

"The Daughters of the Republic of Texas."

"They put this event on every year," Zander told her. "This is my second one."

"Those chairs over there?" The guard pointed to several longer rows set up on another, larger raised platform. "That's for the dignitaries marching in the pilgrimage. Here." He took her arm and led her to a place where she had an unobstructed view. "No one will get in front of you here. But don't move!" he winked at her.

"Thank you very much." Besides, she had Zander to protect her.

People were everywhere, in every kind of dress imaginable. Vendors were selling circlets of flowers, balloons, and other celebration paraphernalia. The air was alive with the sense of festivity. Robin made a firm resolution that next year Bobby would get to see it all.

By four thirty, the area was already jammed, and she had to squeeze her way in between two men to be in a position to take pictures. She was aware that Zander practically had his body plastered to hers. The ultimate bodyguard and protector. No—guardian.

One of the men, the much older one, smiled down at her. "This your first time here?"

"Yes. My nephew is in the hospital, and I want to take pictures for him."

"Here." He stepped back a little. "You just move in front of me. I can certainly see over your head."

"Oh! Thank you so much. I appreciate it."

"Gotta take care of our kids, right?"

She nodded.

"Okay. You'll hear the sirens first. They always get a police escort, so be ready when they come around the corner." He pointed to the left.

"I will. And thanks again."

Zander moved so he was protecting her with his body and wrapped his arms around her from the back. Guardian was definitely the right term for him.

****

Jason Delaware had been irritated when C.D. set the meeting place. He was paying the man an exorbitant fee and wanted to be the one to dictate the time and location. But Ellis wanted to give himself more time to size up the man before getting down to business. They'd only had the one meeting, and he didn't really have a sense of who Jason Delaware was. C.D. had found that watching people interact in a crowd told him a lot about them.

C.D.'s two security people—Frank called them, his well-dressed thugs—were standing at the bar next to him when Jason walked in with his own entourage. Already irritated at having to make the trip downtown in the midst of Fiesta traffic, his mood was obviously tense.

The men shook hands, although anyone watching them would never mistake them for friends.

"I thought we'd have a few drinks down here first," C.D. said, "then go up to my suite and talk."

"This is about the only chance you'll have in here," Jason told him. "As soon as that pilgrimage is over, this place will be wall to wall people. You won't be able to hear yourself think."

But it will be enough time to give me the reading on you I want.

C.D. nodded. "Good thought. What are you drinking?"

"Bourbon. Neat. But just let's not forget what we're all here for, okay?" Jason spat at him. "Saving my ass is the order of the day, I believe."

C.D. gritted his teeth. "Fine, but let's get that drink, shall we?"

* * * *

Robin heard the sirens first, just as the man said. Without leaving her space, she turned and peered onto Alamo Plaza through the rows of chairs and the bleachers set up for Friday's parade. First, she saw the uniformed police on the motorcycles, then behind them the procession, marching four abreast.

They came around the end of the bleachers onto the semicircle in front of the Alamo. The Daughters of the Republic were first, holding their banner. Behind them came the Sons, in navy blazer, gray slacks, and Stetsons. And after them, stretching endlessly, all the genealogy societies made up of families that were a part of Texas history.

As they marched in slow, measured tread in front of the crowd, the sound of a solemn drumbeat echoed from the loud speakers, and a man with a deep voice began to read the names of those who died defending the Alamo. As each group passed in front of the mission, they placed a wreath on the lawn in front of the carved wooden doors.

Robin snapped pictures with her phone as fast as she could, wishing she had a tape recorder to capture the sounds. When the procession ended and everyone had taken their seat, a woman stepped up to the podium to begin the program. Robin saw this as her cue to exit ahead of the masses.

"Thank you very much," she told Patrick, retrieving her car keys from him.

"My pleasure." He touched the brim of his doorman's hat and smiled.

When she tried to tip him, he shook his head. "I'd do anything for the doctor. Glad you got to take your pictures."

But the ringing of his phone interrupted her. Zander punched the button to answer. "Yeah, what is it?"

Robin was still pulling at his arm. "I have to tell you this." She tried to swallow back the urgency. "Please."

His face turned to steel as he listened more in the phone. "Fuck. Just fuck."

"It's C.D." It wasn't a question from Robin. "I don't know how I know this or how he found us, but he's in town. Right?" A chill slithered down her spine.

Zander frowned. "How do you know already? He just arrived today. Guardian's been keeping an eye on the private hangers at Peter O. Knight field in case they somehow headed here, which they did. Now we're going to find out why he's here."

"Zander, he's after me. How did he find me? What can we do?"

"We don't know that he did. This just be a terrible coincidence. Let's let Guardian get into it and keep ourselves invisible. They'll be all over this in ten seconds, and we'll make sure Bobby is well protected." He lifted the phone to his ear. "Yeah, Zak, I got it all. You know what I want. What? Yes. And thanks. For everything.

They made a quick stop in the hotel gift shop to get the T-shirt Bobby wanted before climbing into their car. Robin was so focused on the traffic she was completely unaware of the man hurrying through the door behind her and jumping into an SUV parked at the curb.

****

C.D. was leading Jason through the lobby of the hotel when his eye strayed to the front door and was caught by a woman talking to the doorman. He thought his heart would stop when he spotted her. He couldn't believe it. Robin Fletcher—here? And almost within arm's reach? He couldn't possibly be so lucky as to stumble on her like this, could he? It had to be someone else. After all, what were the odds?

And who was the man with her?

He stopped so suddenly Jason almost ran into him. "You okay, C.D.? You look like you just saw a ghost."

"Maybe I did." C.D. blinked his eyes to clear them and looked at the woman again. The hair was a different color and style, but he'd bet his damn life that was her, standing not fifty feet away. Diamond.

As the man she was with took his car keys from the doorman and turned to climb into their vehicle, he turned to the man standing next to him.

"George, you're still parked at the curb, right?"

George nodded.

"Then get the hell in your car and pull out in front of the one that woman got into. Block her. Don't make it too obvious, but do it right now, before they get away."

George knew better than to waste time with questions. He was out the door almost before C.D. finished speaking.

"Problem?" Jason asked.

C.D. shook his head. "No, actually, I may have just solved one. I just spotted a witness I've been trying to find for weeks, and I've got to go after her. I don't want to lose her again."

"For my case?" Delaware asked.

"I think so," Ellis lied. What else would he tell him?

"Then go ahead. We'll have dinner here. The food is excellent. Call me and let me know when you'll be back. I'll get a table."

"Thanks."

C.D. literally ran for the front entrance, Chuck behind him. George maneuvered the SUV so the man with Robin could pull away from the curb. The moment they did C.D. and Chuck jumped in with him.

"Stick with her, but don't let her spot you," Ellis warned.

"Do I ever?"

****

The SUV pulled out of the garage and into a rare vacant spot on the street.

"What the fuck?" C.D. spat out. "You think Bobby's in the hospital?"

"Anything is possible. Maybe he fell and hurt himself. Or got sick."

"She should be taking better care of my son. In fact, she shouldn't even have him."

George shook his head. "I don't think you're one to be complaining," George told him.

"He's my *son*, you asshole. I'll never let her get custody of him. I own him." No one said a word as C.D.'s words hung in the air. "I mean…"

"I think we all know what you mean, sir. I'm gonna call Frank and fill him in. He'll know what to do."

"And you don't think I do?" C.D. snapped.

"I think this is an emotional situation for you," George said. "But we know where the woman is, and you have a high-profile client waiting for you at The Menger. I'd bet she's not going anywhere so let's use our heads here."

A muscle twitched in C.D.'s cheek. He didn't like not being in control of a situation.

"But where's Bobby?" C.D. pressed. "Is he here in the hospital? And why? And who the fuck is that guy with her?"

"We'll find out all those things," George assured him. "You just need to count to ten and take care of business. How about we take you back to your dinner and we do a little research? I've got the guy's license plate. I can have Melanie do the research. That work for you?"

"One of you stay here and watch for her. Maybe see if you run into her."

"Okay, boss."

"And see if you can find out what the fuck she's doing in San Antonio, anyway. I don't think she knows anyone here, but we have to find out. I'm calling Frank. George, you call Melanie and tell her to get out her shovel and dig deeper into that woman's life. There's a clue somewhere. Let's get back to the hotel, but Fred, you stay here and keep an eye on things. Maybe stroll the hospital corridors again like you're going to see a patient."

"Sure thing, boss," and he climbed out of the car.

Chapter Seventeen

Robin's excitement at getting the T-shirt was dulled by the fact that C.D. was in town. Zak had called Zander while they were on their way to tell them C.D. was here to see a high-profile client, and it was all over the local media. Business never stopped for C.D. She almost felt as if she couldn't breathe, but Bobby was foremost in her mind. The T-shirt would do a lot to raise his spirits.

The hospital, when they were back inside, was buzzing with dinner activity. Robin practically ran into Bobby's room and let out a breath when she saw him eating his meal. All was good. Jim Mercer was sitting next to him and reading to him from one of the books from the playroom. She was pleased to see Bobby's color was a little better, but she wasn't fooled by it. They hadn't even started on the path to healing yet.

Bobby looked up as they walked in then dropped his fork on his plate.

"Did you get it?"

"Of course." Zander grinned at him and removed the T-shirt from its bag, then shook it out for him to see.

"It's the real thing!" he squealed.

"Well, of course it is." Robin laughed. "You think I'd try to pass off a cheap copy?"

"Thank you, thank you." He hugged the shirt to his chest. "I love it."

"I take it the visit to the parade was a success?" They

hadn't even heard Gage come into the room.

"More than," Robin told him. "Thank you for pointing us in that direction and for giving us directions to make it easy."

"A pleasure," he assured them. "Bobby, I've got some good news to share with your aunt and Zander. How about you let me chat with them for a few minutes, and we'll fill you in?"

It was obvious the little boy didn't want them to leave the room, but Robin hugged him and said they'd be back in a minute."

"Okay, give," she told Zander the moment they were out in the hallway.

He didn't mince words but went straight to the subject at hand.

"You're a match, Robin. Right on the money."

Her knees were suddenly so weak she was afraid she'd collapse, except Zander pulled her close to him and wrapped his arms around her.

"Told you, babe. Everything's going to be fine. Gage, when can they do the surgery?"

"We have some more lab work to do, and I have to schedule the operating room and the surgical team, but I'd say no later than a week. Meanwhile, it gives us time to build up his strength. Let me get the paperwork started, and I can tell you better."

"I can't thank you enough," she told him. "Really."

"No thanks necessary. I'm a sucker for happy endings. Now get back to your nephew and tell him we're going to make him well."

Before they walked back into the room, she reached up and pulled Zander's head down to hers, giving him a scorching kiss. "Thank you, thank you, thank you. I am in your debt forever."

He chuckled. "Not really, but I'm happy to take the obligation. It's all going to work out, Robin. Everything, including the situation with C.D. While you're talking to Bobby, I'm going to call Reno and ask him to come by tonight. Now that we're getting this situation under control, we need to make sure the rest of your life is the same. That means figuring out what to do about C.D. Ellis. No more waiting for him to make the first moves."

Robin shook her head. "I hear you, but you know my first inclination is to keep hiding."

He pulled her around so she faced him and tilted her face up to his. "The truth, Robin, which we've been waltzing around while we took care of Bobby, is you can't hide from him forever. We need to find a way to take control of this situation. I'm calling Reno to come by and meet with us after we get home. We need to put a more aggressive plan together. We're missing some things, and I don't know what. But Guardian will find them. Reno had the entire staff working on it."

"Unless you can find proof he killed Milla, I don't see where we can go with this."

"We'll find it, trust me. It's one of the things we do."

****

The first thing C.D. did was call Frank and drop the bomb on him.

"I'm telling you," he all but shouted, "she's here. Right in San Antonio. What the fuck is she doing here? How does she even know anyone in this city? And if she's here, Bobby has to be, too."

"I'll get right on it," Frank told him. "There was never a hint of a connection here so let me see what I dig up."

Desiree Holt

"Dig deep," C.D. snapped. "I want her located and eliminated and Bobby found yesterday."

"We'll find a link," he promised. "You have my word."

How he kept himself together tightly enough to deal with Jason Delaware after the shock of seeing Robin Fletcher was a question Ellis would ask himself later. His mind was whirling, his anger seething. Only the fact that he had Frank on top of this gave him the self-control he needed for his meeting. He had to finish dinner and see what Frank had dug up. Frank could find anything.

Unfortunately, Delaware had more questions than a ten-year-old, and he wanted detailed answers. He was so sure he'd gotten away with something clean. Nothing that would bring a guilty verdict. C.D. thought it ironic he was defending a man accused of killing his wife. He had to play this very carefully. The cops were all over him like white on rice, and Delaware saw C.D. as his only escape route.

Finally, when his patience was exhausted, C.D. excused himself and went into his bedroom with George, who was on his cell.

"Anything yet?" he asked.

Both men shook their heads. "Frank's all over it, though, and so is Melanie. And we're making phone calls."

"Find out who the person was that she checked into the hospital. And what the problem is. If it's Bobby, I can have her arrested for kidnaping."

"Do you really want the cops involved right now?" Chuck asked, his tone edged with skepticism.

No, he didn't. A good point. Chuck was right. Not until he had more information.

"We have to find a way to get her alone. Where the hell is she staying, anyway? And why San Antonio? Why can't we find that out?"

"We're just not looking in the right place. I'm all over this one, I promise you. I'll get answers."

"Don't you want me to hang here with you and Delaware?" Chuck asked.

"No." C.D. shook his head, even though he knew Chuck could not see him. "I hardly think he'll attack me. He needs me to save his ass. Now get going. This is more important."

He wasn't happy half an hour later when George called to report a problem.

"Two things. I think I spotted her taking the elevator to the children's floor, but you need a key card to access it, so it could very well be Bobby. There's no indication she has a kid of her own, and there are no others in the family. You had me check their family tree when you first started seeing Milla. Apparently, they guard those kids like they're royalty.

"Shit, shit, shit." Ellis wanted to pick up something and throw it. This was not going according to plan at all. "Did she spot you at the hospital?"

"No, but she doesn't know us, anyway. And here's another wrinkle. The guy driving the car she was in is there with her, and he doesn't look like anyone you want to tangle with."

C.D. was stunned. "Who the hell could she know like that? Keep an eye on the parking garage. I'm sending George back so you have transportation if you need it. Watch the garage. They have to leave sometime. Let's hope it's not before he gets there."

"I'll figure something out."

C.D. certainly hoped so. This was turning into a real clusterfuck.

"Of all the damn rotten luck." He paced, rubbing his hand across his face. "All right. They can't stay there all night."

C.D. threw the phone on the bed. He wanted to scream, but his client was waiting impatiently in the next room. He had to find Robin Fletcher again. She was the only lead to his son. And then he really would kill her.

****

Robin was so excited she could hardly contain herself. She was a match! She could donate marrow to Bobby and save his life.

"We still have some more lab tests," Gage warned her. "We have to make sure you don't have anything lurking in your body that would be fatal to him or prevent his recovery."

"I'm healthy as a horse," she assured him.

"Horses have been known to get sick," he told her. "We do this with everyone. We'll do the tests in the morning and have the results right away. I'm going to be optimistic, throw my influence around, and reserve an operating room and a surgical team. If everything tests out, we'll do the surgery at noon."

Robin had to clasp her hands as she trembled with excitement. "I can't believe it's happening right away."

"All things being equal. Let's cross our fingers."

"We need to tell Bobby," she insisted. "I need to prepare him, although he already knows he's having a procedure."

"Let's wait until we get the test results tomorrow," Gage told her. "It's only one more day. He's had a big day already, and I think we need to let him get some sleep."

She hated the thought of leaving him, but she knew Gage was right. She insisted on taking the time to read Bobby a story, then hugged him tight as they said their goodnights.

"I just wish I knew why Milla never told me about this," she told Zander as they headed toward the elevator.

"You heard Gage yesterday. The doctor he was seeing may not ever have tested for it unless there were acute symptoms. Even if Milla was the best mother in the world. This shit happens. That's why there are kids in hospitals."

"I know, I know. It's just…"

"But we caught it now," Zander said, "and we're taking care of it. Let's go home, have a glass of wine, and get a good night's sleep."

"You're right. As usual."

When they stepped off the elevator into the garage, she nearly bumped into a man standing to the side. She frowned at him, thinking he looked familiar for some reason. But she didn't know anyone in San Antonio except for Zander, Guardian, Gage, and the hospital staff.

"I'm seeing things," she told Zander when they got into the car. "That man looked familiar, but I hardly know anyone here."

"Maybe it's all the strange faces getting mixed up in your brain, but let's not discount it." He pressed a button on his phone in the cell holder and kept it on speaker.

"Guardian Security." The woman's voice was low and even.

Robin couldn't believe people were working this late at that office, but then she remembered the business they were in. The need for security and investigation didn't stop at five o'clock.

"Hi, Reena. It's Zander. Who's on rotation tonight?" He glanced over at Robin. "We always have two or three people on standby in case something comes up. Which it usually does."

"Dean Lewis and Maria Sanchez. What do you need?" In a lower voice, she asked, "Anything to do with this high-level situation the partners are all focused on?"

"As a matter of fact, yes. It may be nothing, but can you get someone over to the parking garage at my place? I think someone's on our tail, and the best way to check is to see if they hang on until we park."

"Okay. You need anyone else?"

"Just as a precaution, stash someone in the little lot across from my condo building. I'll check in with you when we get home."

"Consider it done. Check in with me when you get home."

Zander disconnected the call.

"It could be nothing but I'm not about to take any chances. I'm going to drive around a little to give our people time to get in place."

Robin clasped her hands together in her lap.

"I can hardly believe this is happening. Do you think there's a way C.D. could have found me here? How is that possible?"

"I learned a long time ago not to discount anything," he told her. "It's how I survived in the SEALs. So let's cover all our bases."

"Zander, listen." She nibbled her lower lip. "I have to say this. I am so, so sorry I dragged you into this mess. I—"

"You didn't drag me into anything. It's what I do for a living." His lips curved in a soft grin. "With some added benefits. Robin, I am doing this willingly. My goal is to make sure you and Bobby are safe. Now, how about a shower and a glass of wine? Your nerves are tighter than an old lady's corset."

She had to grin at that. "Good idea."

Although she was pretty sure it wouldn't relax her until she knew what was going on and if C.D. had somehow tracked her here.

****

"I followed them home," George told C.D., "and watched them enter the garage. It's a ritzy condo building with three kinds of security, so it's not a good place to snatch her."

"What about the guy she's with? Any idea who it is? Or how the fuck she met him?"

"Melanie is tracing the license plate for us. That will at least give us a starting place. I'm telling you, C.D. We have to plan what we do next very carefully. I don't like this situation."

"We always come out ahead," C.D. reminded him. "We will this time. You guys just do your jobs, and we'll be okay. I think I'll fly Frank down here, too. Can't have too much help if what you say is true."

"Good idea. Have him call when he lands, and we'll hook up."

****

Robin was in the shower letting the hot water beat down on her tense muscles and blot out everything else when the door opened and a very naked Zander slid in.

"I called Guardian again. I don't like leaving Bobby with only hospital security so I called Gage and cleared it for Guardian to have a person stationed there."

"I don't want Bobby scared by strangers," she told him.

"Don't worry. We'll get her fixed up as a volunteer and tell Bobby we want him to feel safe when we aren't there so Mona will stay with him whenever we're gone."

"Thank you." She leaned against the shower wall. "And they'll check for any traces of C.D.?"

Zander was silent for a moment, and Robin's muscles tightened and pinched.

"What is it?" she asked. "Tell me. Right now.'

"First, I want to assure you Guardian has this covered six ways from Sunday. They don't take chances with clients. When I called the office back to arrange a guard for Bobby, they had a disturbing piece of information for me."

"Like what?" Nausea crept up into her throat.

"C.D. is in San Antonio to represent a high-profile, mega-rich client for…guess what? Killing his wife."

Robin didn't know whether to laugh or throw up.

"Of all the damn places for him to show up. Zander, what will we do? Can we move Bobby to another city?"

"Take a deep breath," he told her, his fingers kneading the tight muscles at her shoulders. "Moving him will call unnecessary attention to him, and he is medically in the best facility he could be in. We're close to scheduling the surgery, and that would create unwanted complications. Babe, you have to trust me that Guardian and I have this under control. Reno is on his way here, and we're going to draw up a war plan."

She leaned back against him, realizing he was completely naked. Of course he was; he was in the shower…and his very hard, very thick cock was pressing against the crease of her ass. How could this be happening in the midst of a crisis.

"I'd better get out of here and dry off, then."

"He won't be here for another thirty minutes, and you definitely need a tranquilizer to focus on what's happening."

"Is this a time for sex?" How could he even be thinking of it?

"Best thing to take the edge off. I want you not so uptight when we talk. Trust me. It will help."

She had seconds to wonder if showers with women were a regular part of his routine when he began to stroke her with his hands and her brain shutdown. Sliding one hand around to her front, he dipped his fingers into the crease of her sex and began to slowly and methodically stroke her clit. Even in the short time she'd been here, he'd come to know her body and its trigger points well. It didn't take long for him to tease the sensitive piece of flesh to the boiling point and slide his fingers inside her. She knew how wet she was by the ease with which he entered her, and applying his thumb to her clit, it took only seconds to bring her to orgasm.

She leaned back against him, her legs weak, but she had to admit the sharp edge of tension had eased.

"I owe you one," she told him.

"You owe me nothing. I get plenty of pleasure from this. And now, if you can move, I think we'd better dry off and get ready for Reno."

Zanders' phone rang just as they finished dressing, and he punched Talk.

"Yeah. Go for Zander."

"I'm on my way up," Reno told him. "Is it safe?"

"Ha ha. We're all business tonight."

That's a lie, Robin thought, but she had to admit Zander's version of a tranquilizer did more than any pill could have for her.

"Get your ass up here," Zander added, "so we can figure out our next moves."

By the time Robin entered the living room, Zander had brewed coffee and both men were seated, sipping the hot brew.

"We can't let Ellis know we know he's here," Zander started.

"Too late," Reno told him. "It made the afternoon news. His client is a high-profile news magnet who gets way too much publicity. The public has already tried and convicted him of the murder of his wife and people are pissed that this high-value, profile lawyer might get him off."

"If anyone can do it, C.D. can," Robin told them, her tone edged with bitterness. "His specialty isn't proving people's innocence. It's getting them off when they're guilty. That's how he made his fortune. I'll still never see what Milla saw in him."

"Rich. Powerful. Good looking." Reno recited the list to her. "Men like him are the personification of evil, but they know how to put on a good act."

"I can't let him get hold of Bobby," Robin said, clenching her fists in her lap. "I just can't."

"And we won't," Reno assured her. "Listen, I made some changes in the agents assigned to this. I have Chad Fenton monitoring both the garage and the building. He was on the team that just busted that terrorist group in Peru," he told Zander. "You can't fool him even for a second. Lena Holloway is double teaming with him and I've sent Mona to the hospital with Bobby."

"Is she good?" Robin asked. "I mean, I know she must be, but—"

Zander held up his hand. "After you meet her, you tell me. She's our secret weapon. We use her for everything from witness protection to hostage rescue."

"Oh. Well, then. I can't wait to meet her. Should we go back there tonight?"

Reno shook his head. "No. I'm sure they've got eyes on the hospital, and we don't want to give them something to look at if we don't have to. Now, let's get busy with a plan here."

Chapter Eighteen

At six in the morning, the phone rang in C.D.'s suite.

"Nobody's moved in or out since last night," George told him. "It's like they vaporized once they went into the building."

"It's a hospital," C.D. told him. "And they're in there with the boy. But someone's gotta come out sooner or later, or I'll figure out how to rattle some chains."

"Yeah. One can hope." He usually didn't let his irritation show like this when he spoke to his boss. But he was tired from catnapping in his car all night and not in the best of moods. "Want me to go ask them?"

"Don't be a smartass," C.D. snapped. "They have to leave soon. Call me back in an hour." He crossed the suite to bang on the door of the other bedroom. Chuck opened it, running his hand over his sleep-disheveled hair. "Get dressed and come out in the living room. I have a chore for you."

By the time Chuck presented himself, hastily showered and dressed, C.D. had ordered an urn of coffee and breakfast for two.

"Do you have your laptop with you?"

Chuck nodded. Everyone who worked for C.D. carried a laptop at all times.

"All right. I want you to look up the hospital the bitch has Bobby stashed in."

"Are you sure he's there?" Chuck asked.

"Yes, I'm sure. She's walking around so who the fuck else would it be? She better not have let that kid get hurt."

"So what am I looking for?"

"Call the hospital. Tell them you're trying to find your son. Your wife ran off with him, and you think he's hurt and she's not to be trusted. Fancy it up that way you're so good at. Give them his name but tell them she could be using a different one. Go on. Get on it."

C.D. knew if anyone could do it, Chuck could. He had a smoothness to his style that suckered everyone. But as he listened to the man try to work his magic, he began to have doubts. What the fuck was going on that they couldn't get a simple piece of information? He'd have to send Chuck there in person and have him put on a good act.

"Nothing?" he asked when Chuck finally disconnected the call.

"You'd think I was trying to get information about the president. In fact, that might be easier. I need to show up in person. They'll see how concerned I am."

"Be careful," C.D. warned.

"Careful's my middle name."

****

Gage was waiting for them when they arrived in Bobby's room. Jim Mercer was reading in the chair beside Bobby's bed. He rose when they entered and shook hands with everyone.

Robin gave Bobby a hug, with an extra squeeze, and looked over at Gage.

Next to Reno was a woman who wasn't much bigger than Bobby. Robin stared at her. *This* was the protection? Could she even save an ant? But she noticed that both the woman and Reno had badges clipped to their lapels.

Thank you, Gage.

"Let's step out into the hallway for a minute," Reno told them.

"Meet Mona Gillespie," he said by way of introduction. "I selected her personally for this assignment."

She was barely five-two, trim, with her blonde hair pulled back in a ponytail. Her dark brown eyes looked as if she'd seen more of the world than she wanted to.

"Is it true dynamite comes in small packages?" Gage asked Reno.

"Believe me," the woman told him. "I can take on anyone you can throw at me. Your young patient will be very safe with me."

"Well, I have news, too," Gage told them. "We're a go for the bone marrow transplant."

Robin was almost weak with relief. She allowed herself to sink into Zander's embrace for a moment before taking a step back.

"We need to tell Bobby. Gage, will you explain the whole process to him?"

He nodded. "The three of us have already told him it was a possibility, but now we have something definite. Let's do it."

When they walked back into the room, Bobby stared at them, forehead wrinkled, a touch of fear in his eyes. "Did I get sicker?"

Robin sat next to him in the bed and took one of his hands while everyone else gathered around.

"As a matter of fact, you're going to get better," Gage told him. "Remember we talked about bone marrow and I showed you pictures and diagrams?"

Bobby nodded.

"Well, it seems your Aunt Robin is a match for you so we're going to do the procedure today."

His eyes widened. "For real?"

Robin nodded. "For real. And then you will start to get better."

He stared at her for a long moment. "My dad can't find me, can he?"

It was the first time he'd brought up his father since the night they left.

"No, honey. Zander will never let him get near you." She'd kill C.D. herself before she let that happen. "You aren't even listed here under your own name, just a patient number for the clinical trial. Don't you worry."

"I'm going to let you all sort out what needs to be done." Jim Mercer rose from his chair. "Dr. Hollander, you let me know if you need me for anything. This young man is number one on my list right now."

"Thank you," Gage told him.

"We are so grateful to you." Impulsively, Robin gave him a hug. "Thank you so much."

"I lost my grandson to a disease like this. I know what you are going through. This young man fills a hole in my heart and I am honored to be part of this and help in any way I can. Now, let me get out of here so Dr. Hollander can walk you through everything and get things started. Just remember, I'm here if you need me."

"Where do you find people like that?" Robin asked Gage.

"Sadly, the hospital is full of them. People who have suffered the pain of loss and want to help others. Robin, a nurse will be in shortly to give you instructions and start the prep for the procedure." He squeezed her hand.

"It's going to be fine, I promise."

Reno finished giving Mona all the detail she'd need and running through the process with her and what was expected of her. Gage had been at the nurses' station while they were talking, but now he walked back in the room.

"Just wanted to let you know the operating room is scheduled for noon," he told them. "Nurses will be in shortly to start prepping Bobby, And you, too, Robin. Long day for both of you. I'll see you again when we're ready to rock and roll."

Long day didn't begin to describe it as far as Zander was concerned. Reno, special friend that he was, had cleared his calendar for the day to spend it with Zander, and he also kept in constant touch with the Guardian office and the agent staking out Zander's condo. Medical personnel were in and out getting Bobby and Robin ready for the procedure. About mid-morning, Gage called Zander.

"I'm in my office, but the front desk just called to tell me a man is here asking about his nephew named Bobby. Said there's a big custody case going on and whatever Bobby is here for, we have to have his father's permission."

Zander wanted to hit someone. So for sure that had been C.D. and/or his people, and they had spotted Robin. This was confirmation.

"They're pretending to call for authorization," Gage told him, "but you'd better get down there."

Robin had been moved to a separate room, and Zander was sitting beside her bed when the call came in.

"I'm on it," he told Gage.

"What's up?" Robin's voice slurred from the drugs

they had given her.

"Nothing. Gage just needs me to check something. I'll be right back."

He grabbed Reno, who at the moment was in Bobby's room, and told him what Gage had said.

"I'll go," Reno told him. "They don't need to see your face, and besides, you should stay with Robin."

"I want to punch this guy's lights out," Zander growled.

"Happy to do it for you when the time comes. Let me go see what's up, and I'll get right back up here."

Zander paced the entire time Reno was gone, willing himself to stay calm. He checked with Mona what seemed like every five minutes, but he didn't trust that someone hadn't found a way to sneak up to Bobby's room. But Bobby had dozed off and Mona was on guard and armed.

Finally, Reno was back.

"Well?" Zander asked.

"Well. A fancy dressed thug was claiming his son was here, a little boy named Bobby, who was at the heart of a big custody suit. He wanted to see him right then and whoever was with him."

"What did you tell him?"

Reno grinned. "Nothing. When the woman behind the desk pointed me out to him he just shook his head and beat feet out of there. He doesn't want to leave a lasting impression here. But we haven't seen the last of him or any of C.D. Ellis's other thugs, I promise you. Mona will be glued to Bobby except when he's in surgery, and I'll be with you in Robin's room. Got you covered, big guy."

"I owe you for this," Zander told him.

Reno shook his head. "That's what friends are for. Nick's changing places with me for the evening shift, and I'll fill him in on everything."

Chapter Nineteen

Zander had never realized how much time could drag when you wanted it to go faster. He was used to long stakeouts and interminable interviews, but none of them had ever been as personal as this one was. He was slightly relieved when Reno said he'd asked the hospital if he could place a security guard near the desk where the unknown man had tried to get information about Bobby. C.D. Ellis was not a man to give up easily.

Now, he was doing his best to keep his impatience under control. He wanted this all over and done with so he could whisk Robin and Bobby to some place safe until they'd nailed Ellis and he was neutralized once and for all.

Easier said than done.

Surreptitiously, he snuck a glance at his wrist.

"It doesn't help to check your watch every five minutes," Reno joked. "It still only moves sixty seconds at a time."

"I know, I know, I know." He sighed and raked his fingers through his hair. "I'm just not used to…"

"Being this emotionally involved with someone," Reno guessed. "Been there and done that. But the two of them are in the best hands possible. I promise you. And most of that time is taken up with prep. Remember, Gage said the procedure itself only takes about thirty minutes."

At that moment, as if waiting for a cue, Gage walked

into the room, a big grin on his face.

"I hope that look means good news," Zander said.

"The best. It went perfectly. Couldn't have gone better. They're taking both Bobby and Robin to their rooms right now. Give them about thirty minutes, and you can see them."

Zander felt as if a load had lifted from his body.

"Told ya," Reno reminded him. "Let's get you some coffee so you can pull yourself together."

"Check the nurses' station," Gage told them. "I got permission for you to steal from them."

Thirty minutes later, caffeinated and feeling almost light-headed, Zander walked into Robin's room, Reno right behind him. A nurse was just checking her vitals and arranging her pillow.

"She's dozing," the woman told Zander, "but she's doing just fine. Right now, she's sleeping off the medication."

"But everything went well?" he asked.

"It always does with Dr. Hollander," she assured him.

"Nice that my public relations team is working," Gage said, walking in the door. "Rest easy. It all went very well. No glitches at all."

Zander felt relief wash over him so strongly it almost made him dizzy. "When can I take them home?"

"That's always the first question. Barring any complications, which I don't foresee, I'd say three weeks for Robin. I may decide to keep Bobby a little longer, but we'll see how he progresses."

Three weeks. Good thing Reno had set them up with Mona because he wanted twenty-four-hour protection. Someone to be there if he wasn't.

"And Mona stays, right?" he confirmed.

"We'll work out a shift schedule. You can't be in two places at the same time twenty-four/seven. Nick, Zak, and I agreed we'd cover some of it, and no, just shut up with your objections. This is personal for all of us."

"Zander, I'm getting you a place to lie down for a while," Gage told him. "You've hardly slept, and we'll need a hospital stay for you if you aren't careful."

"This recliner looks really comfortable," Zander pointed out. "and I don't want to leave Robin. Not right now."

Gage shrugged. "As long as you get some sleep."

"But first, I want to look in on Bobby, because you know that's the first thing Robin will ask about when she wakes up."

By the time he'd done that and Reno had called the office and also met with Mona, Zander was more than ready for a nap. Guardian had located where Ellis was holding his meeting with his client and assigned an agent to ghost him. He fell asleep knowing he'd done everything he could for the moment about the situation. He leaned back in the recliner and, in seconds, was asleep.

****

C.D. was ready to tear someone or something to shreds. He was finished with his damn client for the day and trying to soothe his nerves with some smooth bourbon when he got more bad news.

Chuck had been stonewalled when he went for information about the kid at the hospital desk, and now, they had an extra guard stationed there. If nothing else was a signal that he was on the right track, that was it. Chuck had managed, however, to snap a photo of the man who came to the desk when the hospital staffer called to get information, and he wasn't too happy."

"First of all, Melanie ran that license plate I sent her. It took her a while because it's registered to a dummy corporation."

C.D.'s eyebrows arched. "Are we dealing with crooks? Wouldn't that be a laugh and a half."

"Worse. She finally tracked it back to a company called Guardian Security, a high-level, low-visibility security organization that handles jobs for everyone from top corporations to branches of the government."

"Well, fuck." A bitter taste surged in C.D.'s mouth. "How the hell did that little bitch hook up with them? This is not good."

"And it doesn't get any better," Chuck told him. "When Robin still lived in Seattle, it seems she was in a relationship with a man named Zander Craig. He's now a senior agent with Guardian. She's been staying with him at his place. That's where we tracked them the other night. C.D., these people mean business. Every one of my contacts I reached out to said stay away from them."

"Just how the hell do I do that when she's for damn sure carrying information that could drown me?"

"Then why hasn't she done it?" Chuck wanted to know. "If the kid's in that hospital, she's probably waiting until he gets over what's wrong. Then she can slip away and reach out to the cops with whatever she's got? Which is nothing."

"I hate to point out that you don't know that for sure. She could just be biding her time until the kid is better, like you said." Chuck took a swallow of coffee. "You don't know what the kid might have seen, either."

"Which is why I need to get hold of him before the

cops do. God knows what they've told this Zander Craig and Guardian. Damn it to hell, anyway."

"Let me dig around some more," Chuck told him. "You've got a hearing coming up this afternoon for Jason Delaware, and he's already called three times this morning. You've trusted me to handle things before. Trust me now."

"This is turning out to be a lot more complicated than I want," Ellis pointed out.

"Complicated' s my middle name," Chuck assured him.

Chapter Twenty

Zander had to admit that sleeping in the hospital recliner left a lot to be desired, but he wouldn't move far away from Robin. He'd also checked twice on Bobby, who seemed to be doing very well.

"He's been sleeping pretty good," he told Gage when he came to check on him while Zander was in the room. "He actually downed some soup and juice, and the nurses say his vitals are good."

"He's coming through like a trooper," Gage agreed. "Let's step out in the hallway for a second."

"What's up?" Zander asked. Robin would be waking up again, and he wanted to be there.

"Can you give me some background on what the hell is going on here? Men looking for information about Bobby and who checked him in here. Strange people wandering around. All this security. Reno Sullivan and Guardian don't come cheap, even if you do work for them."

Zander let out a sigh. "It's a complicated story, and you can't let anyone know."

"It's damn complicated if Guardian's top people are providing protection, and nobody will answer any questions. I need to let the hospital know if other patients are in danger."

Zander shook his head. "No one else has a thing to worry about. We just need to keep Robin and Bobby under the radar."

He gave him a brief rundown on the situation, sticking to the basic details.

"Well. Okay, keep your people here. We want Bobby and Robin as safe as possible, and I'll clear it with the hospital and tell them no information to anyone. Not that they would anyway. Go see your woman now. I'll be in to check on her shortly."

He stepped into the room to check the little boy one more time. Easing Bobby back down to the pillows, Gage had the nurse give the boy a light sedative, and they left Mona sitting with him.

"You sure stepped into an angry hornet's nest, buddy," Gage told Zander.

"I know it, but we're keeping it under control until they can be discharged. Then I'm taking them someplace safe until this is settled. Maybe the Vanetta ranch."

"The media has been full of the Jason Delaware case, and Ellis is representing him. But it still doesn't tell us how he found her."

"Probably yesterday, when we went to take pictures of the pilgrimage," Zander told him.

"Understood. Now you'd better get back to your lady while I take care of business."

****

Ellis was glad to get back to his hotel suite by the end of the afternoon. Delaware wanted him to work miracles, and he was doing his best, but this guy had been even more careless than he had been.

"Well?" he asked, tossing his briefcase onto the couch in the living room. "Anything more?"

"Not more than we already know, damn it. I wish I knew how strong her connection to this Zander guy is. I mean beyond just dating. Maybe she also hired him as a bodyguard. Their information says Guardian does that a lot. If she's also a paying client, maybe we can throw up a roadblock there. Otherwise..." Chuck snapped his fingers. "Maybe her old boss could tell us how tight they were."

Ellis stopped his pacing and stared at the man. "Use your head. After all this time, we call him up and ask him if there was someone Robin knew real well that he forgot to tell us about? Someone that bitch could have turned to and trusted? The first thing he'd do is pick up the phone and call the cops, tell them we're nosing around."

Chuck grunted. "You're supposed to be the distraught father. Isn't that reason enough for you to keep digging?"

"Supposed to be? What the hell does that mean? You think I'm not upset because my son is gone?"

But Chuck knew enough not to voice his opinion. "What shall I say when I call? In case they want to know why I'm asking."

"Do I have to think for everyone?" Ellis resumed his pacing again. "You've done this before. Just keep my name out of it."

Chuck booted up his laptop and began his very tedious search.

At seven o'clock, Jason Delaware and two of his bodyguards arrived for dinner and another session. Ellis drank enough coffee to give him a permanent caffeine jag, and he constantly battled an urge to throttle his client.

"Come on, C.D.," the man said, his face a mask of arrogance. "I know how this works. If we simply pay out enough bribes to the right people, we can make the case against me disappear."

Not that Ellis hadn't resorted to it a time or two before, but the circumstances had been a lot different. This case hinged on discrediting the prosecution's evidence, shoring up Jason's alibi, and proving his wife's alcoholism. It didn't help Ellis's disposition that he saw so many similarities to his own situation or that Jason too often reminded him of himself.

Twice during the evening, he checked with Chuck, only to learn that he still had no results to report. By the time they took a break, Ellis was ready to bite nails.

He had a call into the prosecuting attorney for an afternoon meeting tomorrow and was about to send his client on his way when his cell phone rang.

"I have news, boss," Melanie Jacobs told him. "We got a call from one of our snitches at police headquarters."

"Now what?" He certainly didn't need any more bad news.

"Mac Fontaine, the detective who investigated Mrs. Ellis's murder, and Joel Stetler , the fed who's handling the kidnapping, are heading your way."

Ellis was silent for so long Melanie asked, "Are you still there?"

"Yes. That means they know…"He broke off as he realized Jason was staring at him with avid interest. "Listen, don't leave your desk. Find out when they left and when they're expected to arrive here. And what sent them on this road trip. I'll call you back in a little bit."

"Problems?" Jason asked when C.D. hung up.

"Nothing I can't resolve." C.D. pocketed his phone. "Let's call it a night and get ready for tomorrow."

After Delaware reluctantly let himself be ushered

out of the suite, C.D. poked his head in Chuck's bedroom. "Any progress?"

Chuck shook his head. "Not yet."

"We have more trouble." He passed along Melanie's message.

"Well, hell. C.D., this thing keeps getting more complicated. And why the hell do you think those guys are headed here? You think it's possible the bitch reached out to them?"

"No. Not yet, anyway. They may just have decided to have another go at me." He speed dialed Melanie. "Did you find out that information?" he asked, without preamble.

"No, but our 'friend' is calling me back any minute," she told him.

"Okay. As soon as you know, call me."

"You want to pull George off what he's doing so he'll be at the airport when the plane arrives? He can track them."

"Yes." C.D. clenched his fist. "Tell him to stick to those two like glue but not let himself be seen. I want to know if they are aware she's here and if she's on their list of people to see. We can maybe use that to our advantage. You can bet they aren't coming here to visit the Alamo."

"Okay, I'll handle it." Her voice softened. "Take care of yourself, will you?"

"I'll take care of myself when I get my son back and that bitch is in hell." He snapped the phone shut and dropped it into his pocket.

****

Joel Stetler and Mac Fontaine had taken out their shovels, dug deep, and gotten a lucky break. Zander

Craig, an agent with the internationally known Guardian Security, had called Seattle hot on the trail of Ellis. It seemed Guardian had personal reasons for wanting to see this through. Seattle would take any help they could get.

They had gotten permission to fly to San Antonio to question Ellis again. But...the call from Guardian gave them information on the relationship Robin had with. He was apparently a hot shot agent with Guardian and a good friend to Robin. He didn't confirm that Robin was with him, but it stood to reason. Then hopefully, they might find out more about that night if they could talk to her. That had been a huge stumbling block, not being able to interview her at all. Maybe they had gotten lucky after all.

"You'll have to go through Guardian to set something up," their boss warned them. "I know them, and they aren't anyone to mess around with."

"No problem," Fontaine said. "Been there, done that, as you know."

"Just tread carefully. I don't want this thing to blow up in our faces." He rubbed his chin. "I'm sending a forensics team out to the house again to recheck every square inch of the room where Milla Ellis was killed. Maybe god will be good and there's something everyone, including Ellis, missed. Meanwhile, be very careful. Do everything by the book, or Ellis will crucify us."

"Got it." Stetler nodded and handed a sheet of paper to the other man. "Our plane reservations and our hotel information." His lips curved in a tiny grin. "We're staying at a hotel right next to The Menger. Convenient but a lot cheaper. We figured you'd appreciate that."

"How thoughtful," the man snarked. Then he shook

hands with both of them. "Good luck and check in regularly."

An hour later, they were on their way and headed south.

****

By the time Robin was fully awake from the effects of the anesthetic, Zander was ready to bite nails. But the sound of her voice soothed out his rough edges. Mona had been keeping him up to date on Bobby's progress and had switched places with him a couple of times so he could check on the boy himself.

"You came through it very well, kiddo," Zander told him. "You've still got a stay here at this fine hospital, but Gage says everything went perfectly."

"And I'll be all better now?" Anxiety creased his forehead.

"As long as you keep taking your meds and do what Aunt Robin says, then, yes. Good as gold."

Jim Mercer had also spent a couple of hours with the boy, easing his anxiety and assuring him everything was okay. Now, he shooed Zander out of the room to go back to Robin. He re-entered the room just as she was waking up again, this time more alert.

He went immediately to the side of the bed and took the hand that had no medical equipment attached to it. He smiled at her. "Hey, gorgeous."

She frowned. "I think you need to find another adjective. That one's off the table for right now."

He kissed her knuckles. "It's never off the table, and you're always gorgeous. Especially when you are being a warrior princess and donating bone marrow."

An anxious look flashed in her eyes. "Have you seen Bobby? Is he okay?"

"He's fine. Gage said he came through it like a trooper. I've been in and out of his room, and Mona and Jim are with him right now. In a little while, I'll ask if we can wheel you in there. I think it will do both of you good."

Tears welled in her eyes and trickled down her cheeks.

"How can I ever, ever thank you for this?"

He bent down to brush his mouth over hers. "By staying in San Antonio forever. With me. But we'll talk about that when you and Bobby are both out of here and the situation with Ellis is resolved."

At that exact moment, his cell rang, and he was surprised to see Reno's private number on the readout.

"I hope this isn't bad news," he said when he answered.

"Actually, it may be good," Reno told him. "I got a phone call from the one of the Seattle detectives working on Milla Ellis's murder. He and an FBI agent are on their way here as we speak."

"Yeah? What for? They decide to take a run at Ellis when he's not on his home turf?"

"Something like that. Apparently, they also did a lot of digging, discovered Robin's connection to you, and want to talk to her. You know, they never did have a chance to."

"Because she got the fuck out of town before Ellis could kill her and Bobby, too. So they want to talk to her now?"

"They've been told it all has to go through Guardian, so no worries. We'll manage the entire process."

Zander relaxed a tiny bit. Good. They'd have control over the situation. And maybe something would pop up that the police had missed before this.

"Okay." He blew out a breath. "I want to meet with them first and set the ground rules. And you and I will be with her for every minute."

"Consider it done."

He disconnected the call and turned to see Robin watching him.

"What now?" she asked.

He explained to her abut Reno's call and what was going to happen.

"I don't want to do it here at the hospital," she told him. "When can I get out of here? And will Mona stay with Bobby?"

"Yes, to the second, and hopefully, tomorrow for the first. Gage will check you over to make sure everything's good and then we can check you out of here. Let me set it up, okay? They're contacting the San Antonio police to give them a heads up, and Reno will make arrangements for them to meet with you. He's also doing a check on the cops to make sure they aren't in Ellis's pocket."

She reached up a hand to him. "What would I do without you?"

"I don't know." He grinned. "But I sure don't plan to find out. Now, let's get Gage in here and see if we can disconnect you from all this stuff so you can spend some time with Bobby."

"Yes! That's what I want now that I'm more awake."

As if he'd heard them, Gage walked into the room, grinning.

"My patient's looking good," he said. "Let's make sure it's not false advertising."

Ten minutes later, she was disconnected from all the tubes and monitors, and Zander wheeled her into her nephew's room.

Chapter Twenty-One

At seven o'clock, Reno found himself sitting in a quiet restaurant with two travel-weary cops.

Joel Stetler, the older of the two, had short-clipped dark hair, now showing some strands of silver. His face might have been carved from granite, and what Reno considered the requisite sport jacket, white shirt, and tie covered a lean, muscular body.

Mac Fontaine was slightly younger, with dark brown hair that just tipped the edge of his collar. Like Stetler, he was dressed in a sport jacket, button-down shirt, and slacks. He was heavier than Stetler, but still obviously all muscle, and had "cop" stamped all over him.

The story they laid out for Reno during dinner turned his stomach.

"So that's the long and short of it." Fontaine swallowed the last of his bourbon on the rocks. He stared into the glass. "I don't usually drink when I'm working, but talking about what Ellis did to his wife...well, I needed something a little stronger than ice water. What a bastard."

Reno couldn't agree with him more.

"What I want to know," he said, looking straight at Joel Stetler, "is if this kidnapping bullshit Ellis is screaming about is still in play? And you have to know that's what this is. Pure bullshit."

Stetler nodded. "We consider the source, believe me. Ellis is anxious to put anyone else in the crosshairs. Plus, Robin Fletcher is the least likely kidnapper. We believe she got the boy out of town to keep him away from Ellis."

"I agree. What a garbage can of an asshole. I can't imagine why any woman would want anything to do with him in the first place."

"He has lots of money and, believe it or not, can be very charming. And from what we've been able to find out, Milla Ellis wasn't nearly as savvy as her sister."

"It's obvious she was only trying to keep her nephew safe," Fontaine told him. "But we also need to know if she saw anything that night. Like C.D. smashing his wife's head. She could be trying to keep both of them safe."

"Which she is, with Guardian's protection. We can't expose her. The hospital gives out *no* information, which is why we were able to check Bobby in there."

"Is the kid okay?" Fontaine wanted to know. "Is he sick?"

"He has aplastic anemia and just went through a bone marrow transplant. Robin was the donor. The hospital has a lockdown on all patient information, so even though Ellis sent someone nosing around, they can't get any info."

"But they know Robin's here."

Reno nodded and explained the unfortunate set of circumstances that exposed her to Ellis.

"She's never alone, and they can't get up on his floor anyway."

"We're told we have to work through you," Stetler said. "Apparently, Guardian has some high creds with law enforcement."

Reno grinned. "We do our best." The grin disappeared. "Right now, she can't tell anyone anything. She hasn't been discharged yet, although that will probably happen tomorrow. And she'll be terrified that the information will leak out and somehow Ellis found her and Bobby."

"We'd get killed if that happened, so we'll be doing everything to see it doesn't." He cleared his throat. "SAPD had offered a guard for protection, but I'm guessing Guardian is going to assume that responsibility."

Reno nodded. "You guessed right."

Stetler fiddled with his glass. "Technically, the boy is still listed as a kidnap victim, despite the strange circumstances. You must realize that."

"If you're thinking of trying to take custody of him, forget it. He stays under Guardian's care."

The detectives looked at each other and nodded.

"Fair enough. As long as we are in the loop."

Stetler nodded. "So when do you think we can talk to her? Time is rushing past us."

Reno looked across the table at the two men from Seattle. "Call me in the morning, and I'll let you know when we can set something up. When are you taking a run at Ellis?"

"As soon as we can fight our way past his bulldogs. He'll probably put on his grieving husband and father act again." Stetler exchanged a look with the other man. "Just between us, I'll share with you that we are going over the scene of the crime yet again, with a full crew. There might just be something we missed. And maybe the sister saw something." He looked at his watch.

Reno nodded. "Look. Bobby isn't going anywhere. I've got an ex-cop in his room with him twenty-four/seven. Let's not get him tied up in red tape on top of everything else, okay? The kid's sick and already scared out of his mind. I don't want to make it any worse."

The two cops passed a silent message between them.

Stetler fiddled with his drink for a long moment. Finally, he gave a brief nod. "All right. But I'll have to clear it with the brass, but I don't see a problem."

"When are you guys going to take your run at Ellis?" Reno wanted to know.

Fontaine's lips quirked in a nasty smile. "Tomorrow afternoon. I told his militia, if not, we have a warrant for his arrest, and we're prepared to make it as public as possible."

"You do?"

"No, but I made it sound good." They all rose from the booth. "Talk to you in the morning."

"Count on it," Reno told him. "Meanwhile I need to get going. Gentlemen? I wish I could say it's been a pleasure."

He paid the bill and headed for his car, punching in the code for Zander. "Here's the update."

****

Robin was sitting up in bed when Zander walked into her room with what she was sure had to be his tenth coffee of the day. He was glad to see color in her face and that she was sitting up in bed.

"I just spoke with Reno," he told her. There is a detective and FBI agent here from Seattle, ostensibly to question C.D. again. And see if they can find Bobby and you."

"They know I'm here?"

"Yes. Going to get the T-shirt probably wasn't the best idea. But Reno's on top of it and they've been told to work with Guardian and not make any waves. Points for our side."

We got them to agree to leave things status quo, but they do want to talk to you." He sat on the edge of the bed and took her hand. "But not here. I'll find out when I can liberate you from here and set up a meeting."

"They want Bobby." Her hands started to shake.

"And you. They told Reno a forensics team is going over the entire crime scene again. I don't know what they think they'll find, but they're determined to nail C.D. for this. I say give them whatever help you can. Bobby's safe as long as he's here in the hospital, and I don't have any intention of moving him in the foreseeable future. And even then, we'll take him out to the Vanetta ranch."

"Good."

"I want Bobby in his room and to put up a big Keep Out sign." He sighed. "I guess I can see where they're coming from."

"They've got a job to do, too." Reno walked into the room behind him. "Bobby is technically a kidnap victim, you know." He rubbed his hand across the back of his neck, trying to ease the frustration gripping him. "They filled me in on everything they know, which I know they only did because they are on orders to let us take the lead. They're sure who did this, but they need Robin to tell them herself. And also give them details about what happened to her sister. According to Mac Fontaine, they've had Ellis pegged for his wife's murder all along but haven't been able to collect enough evidence to make a case of it." He blew out a breath. "No wonder you've been terrified."

"And no wonder they're doing a doover at the crime scene."

Damn, but Zander would love to get his hands on Ellis. He couldn't remember the last time he'd felt such rage. Robin had slid down in her bed, and her eyes fluttered closed. He kissed her shoulder, then settled back in the chair. It was going to be a long night.

Chapter Twenty-Two

Robin was a bundle of nerves the next morning. Reno had called Zander to tell him the detective and agent were anxious to meet with Robin and hopefully Bobby.

"I can't hold them off any longer," Zander pointed out. "Right now, they are being very professional and giving us control, but that might not last."

"So what should I do?"

It was an irrelevant question because she knew the answer. And she had critical information that the police needed to pin this on Ellis. She hadn't even told Zander, fearing he'd make her come out of hiding to share it. Would he be upset with her? But if she'd told him, it would have set things in motion that she couldn't control. And Bobby might not have been diagnosed so quickly and had his treatment.

"You have to meet with them, honey. There's no getting away from it any longer."

Nausea swept through her. It was now or never. What would he think when he knew her secret?

"I have something to tell you," she said in a voice that trembled. "Please don't be mad at me, but I kept hoping something would come out and I wouldn't have to be the one to tell. Or C.D. would already be in custody."

"Robin, he can't be in custody until they have

something firm to pin on him. They're going to go over the crime scene again, but I don't know if anything they find will be convincing without an eyewitness account."

"Zander, remember. I saw him kill Milla. "I saw him hit her and smash her head against the dresser. He won't forget that. He has to get rid of me.""

"Okay, that's spilt milk, but it's the reason C.D. is so hot to get rid of you. Let's move forward from here. I'm getting you out of here to a place where you can talk to the detectives. You tell them your story, and then I'm stashing you away until he and his thugs are behind bars with no chance of getting out." A muscle twitched in his jaw. "Any other little tidbits you didn't bother to mention?"

She shook her head. "No, that's it."

"Let me find Gage and see when I can spring you loose from here so I can make arrangements. Are you okay being away from Bobby for a little while?"

She nibbled on her lower lip. No, she wasn't, not really, but she also knew the status quo had to change. Before too long, Bobby would be ready to leave the hospital and they could only hide him away at the Vanettas for so long. Between the two of them, they had the pieces to build a cage for Ellis, and they'd have to do it soon.

She nodded.

"Let me find Gage and see what's happening."

"Gage is right here." The man himself walked into the room. "What do you need?"

"I need to get Robin out of here at once."

Gage looked from one to the other.

"What's changed?" he asked.

"It seems Robin had a little piece of information she

failed to share. We need to move her fast and in secret."

"I can help with that." Reno walked in behind Gage. "Just tell me what you need and why?"

Gage and Reno were as shocked as Zander that Robin had kept such a vital piece of information to herself, but the time for arguing was past. They all agreed they had to move forward quickly.

Reno called Nick and Zak and told them what he needed. Gage did a final exam on Robin and signed her discharge papers. And before she could blink, she was rolled up in blankets on a stretcher and trundled down to the hospital basement. Peeking between the folds of her covering, she saw an electrical service truck with its rear door open. Gently and carefully, Reno and Zander moved her into the rear of the truck. Zander climbed in with her and Reno, in a serviceman's uniform, took his place behind the wheel.

Zander had told her they had set the meeting for his condo, but after that they'd move her some place way out of Ellis's reach. Maybe Reno's home, which she had been told was on six acres outside the city.

****

Ellis took another swallow of coffee and looked at his client.

"They say they have more than they need to go to trail," he told Delaware. "They're convinced they're going to win. And no one's sitting around with his hand out saying he can make it all go away. There's just no opportunity to *fix* anything here, Jason."

"I have all this money," Jason told C.D. imperiously. "Surely, there's someone out there who wants a nice chunk of it."

"Did you hear what I just said? We need to spend

our energies on building the case for your innocence." He wasn't ready yet to mention the plea offer.

"What about that witness you chased down the other day?"

C.D. had to think for a minute to understand the question. Oh, yeah. The day he spotted Robin.

"I told you. It turned out to be a false alarm. We need to rethink how we want to present our case."

It was time to take a very detailed look at the Delawares' lives and find someone, anyone, who would be willing to at least support their theory that his client's wife had either killed herself or fallen off the balcony in a drunken stupor. They needed someone who would swear Jason arrived home long after it happened. *That's* where the fix would have to be. He'd never been above suborning perjury, and he wasn't about to stop now.

The suite was empty when he returned. Chuck left him a note that he'd gone to check out the condo where they'd spotted Robin and the man connected to Guardian. C.D. crumpled the sheet of paper and tossed it against the wall.

Shit. His life was coming apart, and he was running out of glue.

His cell phone rang, and he snapped it open in irritation. Now what? Then he saw George's name on the Caller ID. "This better be good news because I've had all the other kind I can take."

"Our visitors are on the move and their local host is with them."

"They're going somewhere?"

"Uh huh. And I'm going right along with them."

"Just make sure they don't figure out you're tailing them."

"For God's sake, boss. How long have I been doing this?"

"Okay, okay. I'm just on edge. If we don't find this bitch, we're all done for."

"Got it."

"Call me as soon as you know anything more."

He disconnected the call and stuck the phone in his pocket. Restlessly, he paced the room. They were getting close. He could smell it. He couldn't afford to let Robin give the cops chapter and verse. About everything. If he had to sacrifice finding Bobby to get rid of her, so be it. He'd find someone else to give him an heir to carry on his name.

And once Robin Fletcher was out of the way, he could begin to breathe again, live his life. Give his asshole client a defense that would get him off.

Chapter Twenty-Three

The transfer went smoother than Zander could have hoped.

"You make a great delivery driver," he told Reno.

"Maybe I can get a job if Guardian ever closes, although I don't see that happening. Let's get our girl upstairs."

They handled Robin as gently as possible, taking her up in a cart in the freight elevator. Finally, they were inside the condo and Robin was sitting on the couch, pale but little the worse for the wear.

"I guess all this is really necessary," she said in a shaky voice. "I just want to get this over with and get back to Bobby."

"I'll bet you do," she heard Zander mutter. Then he shook his head. "Sorry. Just take a deep breath."

"He's okay, right?" She'd hated leaving him. He was asleep when she left, and she knew he'd ask for her as soon as he woke up again.

"He's fine," Reno said. "Mona's with him, and Jim, and Guardian has another guard on the floor, just in case. But you know how secure that hospital is. And we'll be back before you know it."

"Then I guess let's do this."

In case Ellis had somehow identified the condo in some way, they were taking every precaution possible. Reno had even pulled two of his regular security staff to beef up protection at the condo. Robin had plenty of protection.

The doorbell to the condo rang and Zander checked the door camera to see who was there. Robin blinked in surprise when two men in cable service uniforms walked in.

"Robin, this is Agent Joel Stetler and Detective Mac Fontaine," Reno told her. "They came here to take another run at Ellis, and being able to talk to you after all this time is a bonus."

"No kidding," Zander murmured under his breath.

Robin flinched, wondering if they'd ever get past the fact she'd held out on him.

The men handed her their business cards and showed her their badges, hidden beneath their uniform shirts.

"I imagine you have a lot of questions," she told them. "Please sit down. I hope you understand why I had to run the way I did and stay hidden all this time."

"If you saw something that night," Fontane said, "then definitely yes. But why didn't you come to us before this if you did?"

She looked down at her hands in her lap, tears welling in her eyes. "I saw everything. C.D. killed my sister." When the room remained quiet, panic set in and she glanced at the detective. "You have to understand, C.D. has eyes and ears everywhere. He would have found me and killed me. Witness protection doesn't keep away people like C.D. Ellis." Swiping a tear that fell down her cheek, he glanced at Zander. "I trust Zander without reservation, but I was afraid he'd insist I get in touch with you. I'm sure C.D. has ears at the Seattle police department, and that would have led him straight to me."

"I can't argue with that," Fontaine agreed. "And as much as I'd like to say we could have protected you, sadly, there are no guarantees. Especially with men like Ellis. But We do have a forensics crew going over the house again. Hopefully, we'll find something. Meanwhile, how about giving us your story of what happened that night."

Robin clenched her fists in her lap and drew a breath. She felt a little better when Zander sat down beside her and placed one of his big hands over both of her small ones and gave them a gentle squeeze. Swallowing, she gave them the story of everything she'd seen through the French doors to Milla's room. When she came to the part about her sister's head smashing against the dresser, she almost lost it, but Zander slid an arm around her and pulled her close to him.

"We had a feeling it was something like that," Stetler told her. "No way do you have the strength to hit your sister hard enough, deliver a blow like that, that shattered her skull. But we had nothing else to go on, and you were gone."

Hearing those words made nausea well up in her throat. She pushed Zander away and ran for the bathroom, barely making it before heaving up the small amount of breakfast she'd had that morning. She was leaning against the sink when a knock sounded at the door.

"Robin. Robin, honey, open the door. Please."

He'd called her honey. Maybe all was not lost yet. Taking a deep breath and letting it out, she tugged the door open.

"I'm okay," she told him.

His eyes took in every bit of her from top to bottom.

"Well, that's a big fat lie." He brushed her hair back from her face. "But you will be." He cradled her head in his palms. "We still have to talk this out, but listening to you tell your story to the cops, I can understand why you'd do anything not to have to go back to Seattle. Or put yourself in the limelight."

"I was terrified something would leak and C.D. would find me. Then I'd be dead like my sister."

"Not gonna happen," he promised her. "Even when word gets to C.D., we'll keep you so hidden away no one in his little army will be able to find you. Meanwhile, let's go finish this up."

****

C.D.'s phone rang while he was preparing for his next meeting. He'd been working hard, trying to cobble together a defense for Jason Delaware. He had an unsettling suspicion that Delaware was hiding a drug habit that would turn out to be the reason for his mood swings and his agitation. If the cops didn't know about it, he certainly couldn't afford to let them find out. At that point, he might as well lock the jail cell himself.

He sighed when he looked at his phone, hoping that it wasn't his client calling yet again. The readout showed George's number. A faint shiver of anticipation ran through him. Maybe the man had found something. He'd had him change cars again this morning so he was using a different vehicle every day. One couldn't be too careful.

"Tell me you've got good news for me," he said into the phone.

"I'd say so," George said. "You'll never guess where I tracked those cops to this morning?"

"I'm not in the mood for guessing games," Ellis snapped. "If you've got news, let's have it."

"They went to the condo we followed the Fletcher woman to."

"Shit, they're going to talk to Robin."

"Possibly. They were wearing cable repairman uniforms and came in through the garage. But I had just decided to do a drive through in case there was something going on, and bam! There they were. They think they're so smart, but we're a step ahead of them. I'm dropping Chuck off at that address to see what he can find out. Check when they leave. I can't park for any length of time, but there's a coffee shop in the building across the street that he can watch from."

Damn!

If only he'd gotten to Robin Fletcher before the cops did. For those jokers from Seattle to have hopped on the next plane to San Antonio something had to have turned up. Time to reach out to his secret sources and find out without drawing attention to himself. But he had to get his hands on Robin. Without her as a live witness, it would all be hearsay and he could deal with that.

"If she talks to them and tells them what she saw, I'm dead meat. Although, if all they have is her word, we can do the he said/she said thing. I can tell the cops she's crazy and wants to divert suspicion from herself. I'd love to know what brought those jokers from Seattle flying in here."

"That's key," George agreed.

Ellis began his habitual pacing. His nerves felt sandpaper raw. "Don't go near the hospital."

"But what if she's really there instead of the condo and this is some kind of trick?" George argued. "And the kid's with her?"

"I'll find out without tipping our hand." Although, at the moment, he had no idea how. Everything was turning to shit faster than he could clean it up. He swept his fingers through his hair, excited and frustrated at the same time.

"All right. I'll call you when I find out anything else."

"Fine. But, George? Don't ever make the mistake of underestimating these guys."

He disconnected the call, dropped into a chair in front of the table where he'd been working. He needed a plan. Something workable. And more information than he had.

But first, he'd wait to see what George came up with.

He worked on his notes from his meetings with Delaware. This afternoon he'd have to tell the man he might not be able to avoid prison time. He'd just been too sloppy.

George called him again to tell him they'd kept an eye on the garage, with Chuck watching from across the street. Nothing popped up. Just the usual traffic and each car had its marked space. Delivery trucks and service trucks with no unusual cargo, and that was all.

Three hours later, he was finishing his notes when the phone in his suite rang. What the hell? Everyone he spoke to knew to call his cell phone.

"Mr. Ellis? This is John at the front desk."

"Yes? What is it?" He didn't have time for hotel idiocy.

"There are two gentlemen here to see you. They have law enforcement credentials and say they need to see you. Is it okay to give them your room number?"

No!

He wanted to shout the word. He was in no way prepared to have a cop conversation again. He thought for a moment. "I'm just finishing up something here. Send them up in fifteen minutes."

"Yes, sir. I'll take care of it."

Ellis swallowed the bile flooding his throat, picked up his cell phone again, and dialed a number he'd hoped he wouldn't have to use. By the time there was a knock on the door, he was as informed as he could be and been told who the cops coming to see him were. At least he hoped that was true.

Chapter Twenty-Four

Finally, when Robin and Zander were alone, she felt she could draw a breath, at least for the moment. She insisted on going back to the hospital to see Bobby.

"He's probably already in a panic," she told Zander. "He doesn't know where I went or why. Jim Mercer is doing his best to reassure him, but laying eyes on me is the only thing that will satisfy him."

"No argument here."

Once she was sure Bobby was still safely tucked away and doing well physically, she'd have to sit down with Zander and try to make him understand her sin of omission.

When they got to the hospital, Bobby was sitting cross-legged on his bed, playing checkers with Jim while Mona stood guard over them. He looked healthier to Robin than he had since they'd arrived in San Antonio. Robin gave him a hug so hard, he told her she was squishing his breath.

"Sorry, sweetheart." She loosened her hold but not by much.

Gage came in while she was smoothing the boy's hair and studying him carefully. The doctor had a big smile on his face.

"Good news," he told them. "Today's lab reports are excellent. The transplant took, and the new marrow is working. Another couple of weeks and we should have this young man out of here."

"Couple of weeks?" he shrilled. "I want to go home now."

Gage pulled a chair up to the bed and sat in it, giving Bobby a serious look.

"Okay, kiddo, here's the deal. You know you have a condition in your blood we had to treat. Right?"

Bobby nodded, frowning. "But I thought you already did."

"True, but we need to give everything more time to heal. That takes more than a couple of days. But the tests showed them starting to work right away, so we have to give them time to work completely. We talked about that, too, remember?"

"But how long will that be? I wanna get out of here."

"Of course you do," Gage agreed. "Usual time is thirty days. How about if I set up a calendar on your iPad with something that checks off one day at a time. Every night before you go to sleep, you can check off another day. Will that work?"

Bobby looked for a moment as if he was going to argue, but he finally nodded.

Robin could have kissed the man. She knew, at five years old, a day could seem like forever. This way he would feel as if he had some control over his situation.

"And I'll be here with you every day," she told her nephew until you go to sleep at night.

When I will leave you with Mona or someone from Guardian because I don't trust that Ellis won't try to sneak someone in to find you. He and his top henchmen may be in jail, but there are still telephones.

"Promise?" he asked, his eyes filled with anxiety.

"Pinky swear."

At last, Bobby's face relaxed, and he let Gage show him how to work the calendar app.

"How about if we go down to the playroom?" Jim Mercer asked. "Rumor has it a clown is coming in shortly, and we don't want to miss it."

Bobby's face lit up, and he bounced off the bed.

"Oh, boy. A clown. Let's go."

Everyone laughed as he took Jim's hand and walked out into the corridor.

"He'll be fine," Gage assured her. He frowned at Robin. "But you, my friend, need rest, too. I don't know where you went this morning, but you need to take it easy, drink lots of fluids, and get plenty of rest."

"We had to meet with the detective and FBI agent from Seattle this morning," Zander told him. "They arrested Ellis shortly after that, and they are all on the Guardian plane on the way to Seattle as we speak."

Gage cocked an eyebrow. "You must have had some important information for that to happen."

"Information I should have given before, but I was too afraid he'd come after me and find both me and Bobby." She exchanged a look with Zander. "I'll never make that mistake again. That's a promise."

"Let's hope the situation never presents itself again." He took her hand and squeezed it.

God, she hoped he was over being mad at her. She wanted to start a new life with him and hoped he wanted the same thing.

"It won't," she promised. "Besides, there won't be any more C.D. Elis's in my life. You can count on that."

"Damn straight," Zander agreed. "Okay, let's take a look at the clown and tell Bobby to enjoy the afternoon while I take you home for a well-deserved nap. You still have healing to do, too," he reminded her. "She'll follow your rules," He told Gage in a voice that said that was exactly what would happen.

"There are some meds the nurse has for you," Gage said to Robin, "and scrips to get filled when they run out. I want you on them for four weeks, then we'll do a blood test and see where we go from there."

After saying goodbye to Bobby, Robin did her best to relax as they made their way down to the garage, but she was carrying a heavy load on her mind. Would Zander forgive her? Could they go on from here? Could the three of them make a life together? Would she ever stop looking over her shoulder?

"Relax." Zander helped her into the car. "I'm not nearly as upset as I was."

She felt herself relax slightly. "That's a plus. I wish you weren't upset at all, but I do know why you are."

"I thought you trusted me completely," he told her. "Looking at it now, I can see why you didn't want to do anything to put the spotlight on yourself. I wish you had trusted me more, but I have to believe that trust was there or you never would have reached out to me."

"You're right." She nodded. "I literally put our lives in your hands, and I would do it again. I was just so worried that you'd have to go to the police with what I told you, which is the right thing to do. And then C.D. would find out and send his henchmen after me and maybe kill you at the same time."

He chuckled. "I'm a hard person to kill. I sure don't see this happening again. So let's move on from this and look at the future." He took one of her hands and squeezed it. "I'm looking forward to finally being alone with you again."

"How about a nice hot shower to relax those muscles that are so tight I can see them. Then I think a nap is in order."

"Is that all?" she teased, although tension lined her face.

"It's all until Gage gives the all clear to fully resume your normal life." He winked. "Then I have a lot in mind. Meanwhile, how about that shower?"

****

It was like a three ring circus as it all unfolded. The media had a field day with what they called the downfall of C.D. Ellis. The story was everywhere. A high profile criminal defense attorney being arrested was more than just the news of the day.

"FAMOUS DEFENCE ATTORNEY ARRESTED FOR MURDER"

"C.D. ELLIS ARRESTED FOR KILLING WIFE"

"HIGH-PROFIEL LAWYER BRUTALLY SLAYS WIFE"

Stetler and Fontaine decided it was only fitting to expose the man to everyone for what he was. To that end, they worked with the San Antonio Police Department when they made the arrest. Calls had been made to the local media, so by the time the Seattle detectives arrived at The Menger, a substantial crowd of media had gathered in the lobby, much to the hotel's irritation.

A tip had passed along Chuck and George's location, and they were swooped up at the same time Ellis was arrested.

He was not one to shut his mouth and go along in stoic silence. He cursed the police and everyone near them. Fought against being handcuffed. Swore viciously as he was marched through the lobby and to a waiting police car. Tried to get Stetler and Fontaine to let him make a statement to the police. To those who knew of the nationally famous criminal attorney, he appeared to have lost his mind.

Copies were made of Robin's statement and transmitted to Seattle as well as stored at the San Antonio Police Department. Ellis had demanded to see her face to face, but the police were not having it. As far as they were concerned, she was totally inaccessible and would be until the trial.

Taking Ellis and his thugs back to Seattle became a problem. Commercial transportation was not practical, so Reno offered the Guardian Security plane, using his backup pilot since Zander was glued to Robin's side and didn't appear to be leaving it any time soon.

More media covered the arrival at the Seattle PD police station, and the story was picked up everywhere.

Meanwhile, Robin spent her days at the hospital with Bobby, who improved with each passing day, with Zander always at her side. She would not surface in public until the trial.

Nights were spent at a small inn in northern San Antonio, avoiding the condo just in case Ellis had someone watching it.

"Mac Fontaine told me Seattle has rounded up all of Ellis's cronies who did his dirty work," Zander told her, "but until this trial is over, I'm not taking any chances."

And when Bobby was finally released from the hospital, they took him to the Vanetta ranch, much to his excitement. All of his tests showed the transplant had been successful so he could resume a normal life.

Zander went back to work, but he always had an agent with Robin, who spent some of her time at the

Vanettas. Robin still didn't know what the rest of her life would be like and Zander hadn't brought up the subject. She researched foundations in San Antonio and found a few she wanted to contact when Zander told her it was safe to do so.

Another thing bothered her. She had successfully recovered from donating the bone marrow, but Zander had made no move to make love to her. Oh, they slept in the same bed, and he always pulled her against himself each night. But she wanted to go back to where they were.

Finally, one night, as they lay in bed, he kissed her cheek and nibbled her ear.

"Just so you know," he told her, "I need a lot more than this, Robin. I want it all, but I want to make sure it's what you want, too."

"Of course I do." She wriggled against him. "I thought maybe you didn't want me like this anymore."

"Not want you?" He huffed a laugh. "I've had a lot of trouble making my dick behave, just so you know. Feel this?" He pushed against her so she could feel the hard length of his cock. "I want you more than my next breath."

He slid his hand beneath her long tee shirt, and she grabbed it to press against her breast.

And there it was, the electric zing she got whenever he touched her intimately. "More. I want more."

"Like this?" He cupped the breast and used his thumb and forefinger to pinch and squeeze her nipple. Heat streaked straight to her core, and she had to squeeze her thighs together.

"Yes. Like that. More like that."

He kneaded her breast, teasing her nipple, over and

over again. When her nipple was hard and aching he switched to the other one. She moved against him, pressing herself into his touch.

"I think we need to get rid of this," he told her, tugging up the T-shirt she was sleeping in.

In seconds, she was naked, and he was running his hand over every inch of her skin, tweaking and teasing. She was still spooned against him, but when she made a move to turn over, he pressed his hand against her stomach to hold her in place.

"But I want to touch you, too," she insisted.

"After," he promised.

"After what?"

"After I make you come. Maybe more than once."

At his words, the walls of her sex twitched, and tiny tremors ran though her.

By now her nipples were aching and her sex was needy. She wanted him inside her, but he was determined apparently to set his own pace.

"Please," she begged as he slipped a finger between the slick folds of her sex.

One finger, then two, stroked her until he took her clit between those fingers and tugged and teased it. Her inner walls were quivering with need, and she rocked back against him, urging him to do more and do it soon.

She reached behind her and closed her fingers over his cock, but he nudged her hand away.

"Do that and it will be over in seconds. I've been hard as nails all these weeks, and my hand is no substitute for you and the real thing."

"I want you inside me," she told him.

"Like this?" He slid the two fingers into her wet, waiting flesh.

"I want your cock," she begged. "Pease, Zander. It's been so long."

"I hope it isn't over before it starts. Let me get some protection." He gave a tiny laugh. "I've been keeping it close by waiting for the right moment. For you to finally relax."

He rolled to his back for a moment, reached into the nightstand drawer, and in a moment, she heard the tearing of foil, felt his movements as he rolled the latex onto his dick. Then he lifted her leg and draped it over his thigh so she was completely open to him. The head of his cock nudged against her opening, and she wanted to scream when he stopped.

"More," she cried. "I want it all."

"If you want it all, you have to marry me." His voice was deep and serious.

Robin was stunned. "M-Marry you?"

"Uh huh. As soon as possible."

Joy and excitement mingled with the desire building inside her.

"Well?" He nudged a little more. "I need an answer."

"Yes, I'll marry you. As soon as possible."

He pushed his hips forward. She was so wet inside that he slid effortlessly into her, despite how swollen his dick had become.

"Okay, then. And we'll work on making Bobby a part of our family, too. But first this."

He drew his hips back and, with one thrust, seated himself deep inside her body. They were both so ready that it barely took seconds before the orgasm began to build.

And then they were there, Zander's hand pressed

against her stomach to hold her in place while he pounded in and out of her. The orgasm exploded. Her inner walls spasmed again and again as his thick shaft pulsed inside her.

When the last twitch of muscle faded away, they lay there, spent but satisfied. At last, Zander climbed out of bed to dispose of the condom. Then he was back spooning against her again.

"Soon," he told her.

"Soon what?"

"The wedding. I don't want to wait a minute longer than I have to."

"Okay. We can discuss it." She paused. "After."

"After what?"

"We do this again." She laughed as she turned over and opened her body to him.

This had been such an arduous journey to get to this point, but she knew one thing. She'd definitely won the prize.

A word about the author...

USA Today best-selling and award-winning author Desiree Holt writes everything from romantic suspense and contemporary on a variety of heat levels up to erotic, a genre in which she is the oldest living author. She has been referred to by USA Today as the Nora Roberts of erotic romance and is a winner of the EPIC E-Book Award, the Holt Medallion, and a Romantic Times Reviewers Choice nominee. She has been featured on CBS Sunday Morning and in The Village Voice, The Daily Beast, USA Today, The (London) Daily Mail, The New Delhi Times and numerous other national and international publications.

~*~

Visit Desiree at
www.desireeholt.com